An Amateur Performance

(Reminiscences of a Student in the 1850s)

Lev Levanda

An Amateur Performance

(Reminiscences of a Student in the 1850s)

Lev Levanda

Edited by
Brian Horowitz

Translated by Hugh McLean,
with Conor Daly

BOSTON
2022

Library of Congress Cataloging-in-Publication Data

Names: Levanda, L. O. (Lev Osipovich), 1835-1888, author. | Horowitz,
    Brian, editor. | McLean, Hugh, translator. | Daly, Conor, translator.
Title: An amateur performance : (reminiscences of a student in the 1850s) /
    Lev Levanda ; edited by Brian Horowitz ; translated by Hugh McLean,
    with Conor Daly.
Other titles: Jews of Russia & Eastern Europe and their legacy.
Description: Boston : Academic Studies Press, 2022. | Series: Jews of Russia &
    Eastern Europe and their legacy | Includes bibliographical references.
Identifiers: LCCN 2022029731 (print) | LCCN 2022029732 (ebook) |
    ISBN 9798887190174 (hardback) | ISBN 9798887190181 (adobe pdf) |
    ISBN 9798887190198 (epub)
Subjects: LCSH: Jews—Russia—Fiction.
Classification: LCC PG3467.L435 A83 2022 (print) | LCC PG3467.L435 (ebook) |
    DDC 891.73/3--dc23/eng/20220815
LC record available at https://lccn.loc.gov/2022029731
LC ebook record available at https://lccn.loc.gov/2022029732

ISBN 9798887190174 (hardback)
ISBN 9798887191010 (paperback)
ISBN 9798887190181 (adobe pdf)
ISBN 9798887190198 (epub)

Cover design by Ivan Grave
Book design by Tatiana Vernikov

Published by Academic Studies Press
1577 Beacon St.
Brookline, MA 02446
press@academicstudiespress.com
www.academicstudiespress.com

Contents

Acknowledgements

I am deeply grateful to Hugh McLean, Berkeley Slavist and brilliant wordsmith and literary scholar, who was willing to render the story into English, as well as produce sensitive notes to aid the modern reader. I am grateful to Mr. Conor Daly of Dublin, who stepped in to edit the translation and complete Hugh's effort. I am also grateful to William Craft Brumfield, mentor, friend, and colleague, the author of the preface here. I want to acknowledge the reader of this project, Alice Nakhimovsky; Maxim D. Shrayer, editor of the book series Jews of Russian and Eastern Europe, and Alessandra Anzani, editorial director, both at Academic Studies Press, with all their staff; as well as the staff at Indiana University Press, which has permitted me to use my 2020 article that appeared in *Prooftexts*. I also want to acknowledge help finding photographs of Levanda from Lyudmila Sholokhova and Zachary Rothbart.

 I want to acknowledge the generous help that I received for this and other projects from my Doktorvater Dr. Hugh McLean and his wife Katherine (Kitty), who were close friends and whom I miss deeply. I also want to recognize the University of California, Berkeley, where I first fell upon Russian Jewish literature and started off on a path that still unfolds before me in my seventh decade of life.

On the Translation
Very few of Levanda's works have ever been made available in any language other than Russian (with the exception of Maxim Shrayer's translations) and I do not have any significant explanation for having chosen this story for translation except that it's a charming slice of life that gives a rich portrait of Jewish intellectuals in Russia at the end of Nicholas I's reign.

On the Translator
Hugh McLean (1925-2017) was professor of Slavic Languages and Literatures at the University of California, Berkeley. He was a polymath and brilliant linguist and literary scholar. For additional info, see the article about his career: http://slavic.berkeley.edu/people/hugh-mclean/

On the Translation Editor

Mr. Conor Daly teaches in the Department of Russian and Slavonic Studies at Trinity College, Dublin, Ireland. He got his PhD from UC Berkeley in 1994. His translations have been published widely.

On the Scholar and Book Editor

Professor Brian Horowitz is the author of six books, including *Vladimir Jabotinsky's Russian Years* (2020), *The Russian-Jewish Tradition* (2017), *Jewish Philanthropy and Enlightenment in Late-Tsarist Russia* (2009), *Empire Jews* (2009), and *Russian Idea—Jewish Presence* (2013). He has won numerous scholarly awards and grants. He received his PhD from UC Berkeley in 1993. He holds the Sizeler Family Chair and is a professor of Jewish Studies at Tulane University in New Orleans.

On the Writer of Our Preface

Professor William Brumfield is a Sizeler Professor in Jewish Studies and German and Slavic Studies at Tulane University. He is the leading specialist on Russian architecture worldwide. He studied with Hugh McLean, receiving his PhD from UC Berkeley in 1973.

—Brian Horowitz

Preface

William Craft Brumfield

It is a pleasure to write the preface for this book by, and about, Lev Levanda—the most important Jewish writer in the Russian language between 1860 and 1887, the author of novels and editorials about the fate and future of Russia's multimillion-strong Jewish population. I would like to mention important details that illuminate the book's genesis and goals. But first, let me say a few words in praise of Brian Horowitz, the editor of this volume and my colleague at Tulane University.

Horowitz did his doctoral work at the University of California, Berkeley, and I can say without exaggeration that he developed the previously nonexistent field of Russian Jewish culture. When Brian was at Berkeley in the 1980s, there was little recognition of Russian Jewish literature as a legitimate field. Russian scholarship in the field had ended in the late 1930s, when the Communist authorities prevented scholars from publishing on, and gaining academic promotion through, Jewish subjects. Archives remained shut, and there were no relevant courses or institutions in Russia. The brilliant émigré generation of the interwar period had passed away, and the study of Russian Jewish literature was relegated primarily to religious seminaries. Professional writers knew the work of Isaac Babel and little else. In short, Russian Jewish culture was not a promising subject for a budding scholar.

Fortunately, Horowitz realized that the generational break and the absence of recent scholarship offered a chance to right a historical injustice and rejoin Russian Jewry to Jewish history. Trained as a Slavist, he understood that Russian Jewish culture was sui generis, profoundly enriched in the nineteenth century by the Golden Age of Russian literature (Pushkin, Dostoevsky, Tolstoy, Chekhov). Horowitz deserves great credit for his discoveries, which underly numerous articles and books such as *Empire Jews, Jewish Philanthropy and Education in Late-Tsarist Russia, Russian Idea—Jewish Presence*, and *The Russian Jewish Tradition*. These publications represent the development of an entire field of study. For example, the book before us emerged from Horowitz's plan to compile translations of Russian Jewish stories for a large volume that would lead to extensive translations of Levanda's work. Although that idea did not materialize, it led to the translation of the present story with an incisive introduction that brings Levanda to an English-speaking audience.

In 1995, Shimon Markish, a leading scholar of Russian Jewish literature, wrote an essay entitled "Is It Worthwhile to Reread Lev Levanda?" This question remains. Levanda dealt with existential problems facing Russia's Jewish population: modernization, economic dislocation, violence, and, especially, russification—the idea that Jews needed to integrate into Russian society, learn the language, and appreciate and contribute to its culture, as Levanda had done through his writing. Before the pogroms of the early 1880s, Levanda had shown positive aspects of russification. His literary characters were types who embodied the goals of contented Jewish citizens of Russia: the young intellectual, kind-hearted parents, budding musicians, and generous entrepreneurs. He also warned against the sacrifice of ideals for the sake of money. Levanda was seen to embody this ideal synthesis and he advocated for it: he was a Jew who was fully Jewish and fully Russian, a person capable of discussing Talmud and Pushkin. To some extent, this ideal remains to the present.

In the early 1990s Horowitz asked Hugh McLean to translate "An Amateur Performance." McLean willingly accepted the offer, thus making his own contribution to Russian Jewish culture. Anyone who had the privilege of being a graduate student in the Slavic Department at Berkeley during the last third of the twentieth century and the beginning of this one can remember the pleasure of Hugh McLean's company. I, for one, enrolled in or audited every course he offered during those hyperactive years of the quarter system in the late 1960s. It wasn't simply that he was an outstanding teacher. Everyone in the Slavic Department was superb, at least in my experience. McLean entered a finely honed system for pedagogy and research, and he made it his own, amplifying the work of his distinguished colleagues.

I should emphasize the easy rapport that McLean and his fellow Slavicists had with the History Department (also in dear Dwinelle Hall), whose Russian specialists did so much to define the field in this country. And there was his role as a dissertation adviser—supportive, tactful, not interfering when there was no need. Hugh and his colleagues provided the aspiring scholar with intellectual space at a time when egos were fragile and self-doubt plentiful.

All of the above could be repeated by many who encountered McLean during graduate studies. But for me, the defining moment occurred in the departmental office one afternoon in the spring of 1970. I was checking my mailbox when Hugh came up, tapped me on the shoulder, and asked if I was interested in going to Russia in the summer. He explained that the summer institute

William Brumfield at Dwinelle Plaza, June 1966. In background: Wheeler Hall and Campanile. Photograph courtesy of William Brumfield Collections.

Sproul Plaza meeting, fall 1967. In background: Sproul Hall. Photograph: William Brumfield. Courtesy of William Brumfield Collections.

of the IREX US-USSR Exchange of Language Teachers at Moscow State University was under-enrolled, and there might be a place for me, although, I was not yet an accredited teacher of Russian—only a graduate student with limited classroom experience. In those years US scholars at every level traveled to Russia through negotiated study programs; and gaining admittance to the IREX program, sponsored by the International Exchange and Research Board, was a defining moment, a breakthrough in my still tentative career.

Whatever the logic of my inclusion, those first summer months in the Soviet Union expanded my vision of Russia in a most literal way, and I have never forgotten Hugh's essential role. His thoughtfulness and ability to discern the "le moment décisif" were transformative. No one could have foreseen it, yet that first summer—my first experience photographing in Russia—laid the foundation for all that I was subsequently to do as a photographer and a historian of Russian architecture.[1]

In his later years, Hugh followed the frequent publications in my "Discovering Russia" series and often wrote to me with comments. He was among those who most clearly understood the significance of my photographic project, and I was gratified that he could see some of the results. Was he aware of his propulsive role? I doubt that it occurred to him; those of his standing have little need to claim credit for others. Might there have been alternative scenarios? There usually are, but for me, it will always be McLean's call.

New Orleans, July 2021

---

1   For more on that pivotal period, see "Faded Glory in Full Color: Russia's Architectural History: Interview with William Craft Brumfield," *Kritika: Explorations in Russian and Eurasian History* 17, no. 2 (Spring 2016): 379–404.

Introduction

Brian Horowitz

Lev Levanda (1835-88) is still barely known in the English-speaking world. His famous novel from 1873 *Seething Times* (*Goriachee vremia*) has still not been published in its entirety, although a section has appeared in Maxim Shrayer's wonderful translation in *Polin* (2007) and in his anthology of Russian Jewish literature (1915).[1] Thanks to Levanda's major role in different areas of Jewish culture and politics in nineteenth-century Russia, scholarship in English on him is well represented (see Wikipedia, "Lev Levanda").[2] In this essay, I hope to re- late the drama of his life as it unfolded in the context of Russian Jewish history, as well as discuss *An Amateur Performance*, the novella published in English here for the first time.[3]

Levanda devoted his life to the Russification of Russia's Jews. By Russifi- cation he understood the use of Russian language and integration of Jews into Russian society, its economy, and culture. To a degree, Russification succeeded; by the century's end, many Jews spoke Russian and were involved in Russian life and culture. However, the Jewish response, the government's behavior, and the attitudes of the Russian people did not cohere with Levanda's ideals. Beginning

---

1   Maxim D. Shrayer, "A Selection from Part 1 of Lev Levanda's Seething Times," *Polin: Studies in Polish Jewry* 20 (2007): 459-472; also in M. Shrayer, ed., *An Anthology of Jewish-Russian Literature: Two Centuries of Dual Identity in Prose and Poetry* (London: Routledge, 2015), 39-56.

2   Among the best known works on Levanda are Gabriella Safran, "Lev Osipovich Levanda," in *YIVO Encyclopedia of Jews in Eastern Europe*, 2 vols., ed., Gershon Hundert (New Haven: Yale University Press, 2008); Zsusza Hetény, *In a Maelstrom: The History of Russian-Jewish Prose* (Budapest: Central European University Press, 2008); John Klier, "Jew as Russifier: Lev Levanda's Hot Times," *Jewish Culture and History* 4, no. 1 (2001): 31-52; Maxim Shrayer. "Gaining a Voice, 1840-1881: Lev Levanda," in Shrayer, *An Anthology of Jewish-Russian*, 39- 56; ChaeRan Freeze, "The Politics of Love in Lev Levanda's Turbulent Times" in *Gender and Jewish History*, ed. M. Kaplan & D. D. Moore (Bloomington: Indiana University Press, 1911), 187-202.

3   *An Amateur Performance* appeared in Russian as *Liubitel'skii spektakl'* (*vospominaniia shkol'nika piatidesiati godov*) in *Russkii Evrei*, from issue 11, March 24, 1882 to issue 23, June 9, 1882

as a passionate fighter for Jewish integration, he finished in a sanatorium near St. Petersburg, having lost his mind. Little in Russia's contemporary history had gone according to his expectations; his overblown hopes had dissipated like deflated balloons. His life trajectory appeared not as progress, but as its antithesis. Instead of the victory of enlightenment, he succumbed to the forces of intolerance, chauvinism, and antisemitism.

However, Russification ultimately won out and Levanda's goal was achieved, although the struggle was not easy. Decades before such famous Jewish writers as Osip Mandelshtam and Isaac Babel rose to prominence, there were Jews who lived in Russia and wrote in Russian. What sounds perfectly natural—to live in Russia and write in Russian—was, in fact, quite uncommon. In the first half of the nineteenth century, Jews spoke Yiddish, and educated clergy (rabbis) and community leaders wrote mainly in Hebrew or Yiddish. Knowledge of Russian was often a profession—a member of the community was tasked with recording in Russian the births and deaths of Jews (keeping the official metric book). Thus, the Russian language was not widely used by Jewish subjects of the empire.

In fact, Russian language was not a required subject. Jews lived among non-Russians in the country's western regions, and so communication occurred in Ukrainian, Polish, Lithuanian, or Latvian. Sometimes non-Jews learned a bit of Yiddish.

By the 1840s, incentives appeared for Jews to acquire proficiency in Russian. Two processes began at once: Jews began entering the liquor trade, and the government pursued a program to teach Russian to a few Jewish children. Tsar Nicholas I created special schools for Jews and two state-sponsored rabbinical seminaries in Vilna and Zhitomir.[4] Gradually, opportunities in government service, commerce, and banking appeared for Jews who knew Russian. A bit earlier, the government reorganized the liquor trade, granting monopolies to large producers. A Jew, Gavriel Gintsburg, paid to obtain a liquor franchise, and he hired other Jews to help. Ultimately, around five thousand people were employed. Here Jews needed knowledge of Russian to successfully carry out the business.[5]

Learning Russian wasn't easy. There wasn't a textbook, nor was there a literature in Russian for Jews. It wasn't until 1860 that *Rassvet*, the first Jewish

4   Michael Stanislawski, *Tsar Nicholas I and the Jews: The Transformation of Jewish Society in Russia, 1825-1855* (Philadelphia: Jewish Publication Society of America, 1983).

5   Brian Horowitz, *Jewish Philanthropy and Enlightenment in Late-Tsarist Russia* (Seattle: University of Washington Press, 2009), 17-28.

newspaper in Russian, was given permission to open. One of the founders (and featured writers) was Lev Levanda, whose novella *An Amateur Performance (Reminiscences of a Student in the 1850s)* portrays the first generation of Jews enrolled in the Russian government's Vilna Rabbinical Seminary. Like many of Levanda's works, it depicts a Jewish (male) consciousness at a specific historical moment, the early 1850s, when Tsar Nicholas I wanted to modernize the country. He did so with techniques borrowed from Western Europe—establishing Jewish schools, dissolving the Kahal and communal structures, hiring Jews in the government—but in Russia, such reforms had an oppressive dimension, causing pain, not relief.

Levanda does not give a history lesson. He offers a personal story within a specific context. His first-person narrator recounts the life of a young man, a high school age Jewish student—Levanda himself or a character based on him—who agrees to write a play for an end-of-year event. His comrades, aware that such initiatives are forbidden in Russian schools, try to keep it secret. However, the school officials find out. The young man is exposed.

The plot follows the narrator's relations with the school inspector, the teachers, and the students, as well as his education and the art of writing itself. In a sense, the story resembles Joyce's famous *Portrait of the Artist as a Young Man*. To be sure, the bildungsroman (novel of education), as told from the youth's perspective, was widely popular during the nineteenth century.

The author poses an ideological question (one he often returned to in his work): Where should a Russian Jew orient himself, culturally speaking, between Polish and Russian culture? Polish is the superior culture, and until recently, Vilna— the locus of the story, and Levanda's home—orbited around Poland. But by the middle of the nineteenth century, politics, power, and the Jewish future had arrived in the Russian state, despite its antidemocratic structure and suppression of individual creativity. The novella treats the problem of Russia's heavy-handed government for a modern Jew seeking a forge a bond with Russian culture.

Although largely forgotten (except by scholars of Russian Jewish culture and history), Levanda was the leading proponent of the Russification of Russia's Jews. Since the majority of the world's Jews lived in the Russian Empire (over four million in 1882, when the story appeared), we need to recover his role to understand properly the history of Jews in Russia. Who was Lev Levanda?

Levanda was born in Minsk in 1835 to a poor Jewish family. He attended an elementary school run by David Aaronovich Lur'e, a Maskil (enlightener) who believed that Jews needed to rely on themselves (as opposed to the government) to foster secular education among their own. He established a Talmud Torah (elementary school for poor families) that gave children access to basic skills and access to further education.

In 1846, Levanda transferred to the newly established (1844) government Rabbinical Seminary in Vilna. The name shouldn't confuse one; it was not a Yeshiva or traditional religious institution. The seminary was modeled on German schools that aimed to produce modern rabbis and community leaders who could read and write in German and possessed Jewish as well as secular knowledge. The Russian government created two such schools, one in Vilna, Lithuania, and one in Zhitomir, in Ukraine. However, the government was serious about changing the rabbinate and sought to replace the so-called "spiritual rabbi" with this new-fangled "state" rabbi by insisting that communities pay the latter's salary. Since most communities preferred to retain the original rabbi, they were obligated to pay two rabbis (the dual rabbinate). The "state" rabbi was an expense that few communities relished.[6]

Admittedly, most graduates of the rabbinical seminaries did not work as rabbis; instead, they found state employment as book censors, advisers, and teachers in the growing number of state Jewish elementary schools. Often, graduates went on to medical school or legal studies; a degree from a Russian university or trade school gave Jews the right to live in Russia's capital cities (outside the Pale of Settlement), where they enjoyed financial advantages and escaped the problems that Jews faced in the Pale of Settlement.[7] Another growing industry was in journalism. Levanda chose a writer's career.

Although the story published here appeared in 1882, during the "Spring Storms," the pogroms of 1881–82, we need to go back to the 1860s to discover Levanda's origins as a writer. In doing so, we can understand the context for this story and his fiction overall.

Levanda in the 1860s: Radical Maskil (Intellectual)

In 1860, the tsarist government gave Osip Rabinovich, a well-known Jewish writer, permission to publish the first Jewish newspaper in the Russian language. Although he already had permission to publish in Hebrew or Yiddish, Rabinovich

---

6   On the dual rabbinate, see ibid., 128-130.

7   Genrik Sliozberg, *Baron G. O. Gintsburg: Ego zhizn' i deiatel'nost'* (Paris: n.p., 1933).

had waited. He wanted a Russian-language audience, the better to bring the Haskalah (Jewish Enlightenment) to government officials and the business elite, and thus promote tolerance toward Jews and Jewish integration into Russian society.[8] Although Rabinovich lived and published his paper in Odessa, he envisioned a newspaper that dealt with questions affecting Jews throughout the country, especially the vast majority that lived in the Pale of Settlement. Contributors to *Rassvet*, who wanted to change Jewish society, wrestled with how much to criticize traditional Jewish life. One was encouraged to point out flaws, but not undermine its legitimacy.

The Haskalah in Russia had several unique dimensions. In the Pale of Settlement, Jews were a large minority, comprising around 3.5 million Jews and making up 30-50 percent of the urban population. While Western Europeans were gradually gaining equal rights, Jews in the Russian Empire were still subject to onerous rulings and policies. Jewish integration was minimal; the Russian government discriminated against its Jewish population. Furthermore, the Ukrainians, Belorussians, Lithuanians, Latvians, and Poles who lived among Jews were not eager to accept Jews as equals (as minorities, they were also objects of discrimination). Generally speaking, the conditions of a secular civic society did not exist. In Russia, officially recognized corporate bodies like merchants, Jews, and Muslims still existed, although they were partially hidden by modern identities approximating, but not exactly consonant with, Western notions of citizenship.

However, Maskilim (leaders of the Haskalah) were characteristically radical in their ambitions. They called for immediate and full integration, Russification, increased economic productivity and religious reform. Simultaneously, their hostility toward the rabbinate, community leadership, and the structure of the Jewish community was deep and abiding. In the early period (1820-70), Maskilim expressed nearly unlimited love for the Russian government and imagined a utopian future—the unity of Jews and Russians.

Levanda helped establish the newspapers *Rassvet* and its sequel *Sion*, which was published in Odessa from 1860 to 1862. Levanda especially used the genre of feuilleton because it permitted him to discuss issues that mattered to him in a lively and personal way.

---

8   See Vasily Schedrin, *Jewish Souls, Bureaucratic Minds: Jewish Bureaucracy and Policymaking in Late Imperial Russia, 1850-1917* (Detroit: Wayne State University Press, 2016).

The first issue of *Rassvet* ran on May 27, 1860. There appeared, along with a note from the editor promising loyalty to truth above all else, a feuilleton by Levanda titled "Several Words on the Jews of Russia's Western Province." Levanda presented what might have been the sharpest criticism of Jewish life ever print-ed. Visiting Igumen, a small town in Belarus, Levanda found nothing to praise; everything is bad; the Jews are immoral, rotten, diseased. "Oh my God, what poverty!" he exclaims. "What material and moral degradation!"[9]

Levanda expresses a dislike of gender roles in traditional Jewish society. It angers him that women, never men, work in shops, and fight with one another over prices, thus undercutting their collective well-being. He opposes men's ab-sence from economically productive professions. Instead of earning money for their children, they sit in study houses, hunched over the Talmud.[10] There the Jew gets some consolation and "forgets that his hut is not heated, that his chil-dren went to sleep without dinner, do not have breakfast today, that his wife is unable to bring relief to her mouth burnt from fever, that the landlord threatens to throw his family into the street every day, and the communal authorities have taken his last pillow for lack of payment."[11]

Extreme poverty irritates Levanda. He releases his bile:

> One has to see for oneself, one has to enter a crowded, half-dilapidated hut, which always houses no less than three families, which compete among themselves for the prize of poverty. One has to see how the half-naked children of all three families crowd around the unheated oven and fight over a piece of animal skin, which each child wants to wrap around himself to warm his body, freezing from the cold. One has to be there when the father of one family arrives at the door with a loaf of bread and his children jump off the oven with shouts of joy, singing and clapping their hands together. The children of the other families, whose fathers have not brought food, turn away their eyes so as not to see their com-rades' happiness, which was not to be theirs.[12]

Levanda presents the Jewish family as shameful proof of moral degradation. Their way of life produces a litany of problems: "disorder, unsanitary conditions,

---

9   Lev Levanda, "Neskol'ko slov o evreiakh zapadnogo kraia. Pis'ma v redaktsiiu (Iz goroda Igumena, Minsk[oi] guber[nii]," *Rassvet*, May 27, 1860, 7.

10   Such gender distinctions were typical of Russian Maskilim.

11   Levanda, "Neskol'ko slov o evreiakh," 9.

12   Ibid., 8.

illnesses, poverty and the bad education of local Jewish children; you will not find in another people in any country so many hunchbacks, stooped, crippled and ugly people as I have seen among the local Jews."[13] Although his subject is religious Jews, his intended reader is someone like himself, a Maskil, who can finally face the truth openly and boldly. If you're like me, he seems to say, you will be revolted by Jewish life in Russia.

One can imagine his readers' reactions, and indeed, the response came quickly. In issue seven, Rabinovich published a letter from a group of Jews from Igumen, Zhelezograd, and elsewhere in the Minsk Province.[14] They recalled their joy upon hearing that a Jewish newspaper had been conceived and would soon be published. They recalled that Levanda had once defended Jews in a Russian journal from a false accusation.[15] They wondered if Levanda had written the article quickly, without giving proper thought to what he was saying. Then came the axe. The letter's author (writing on behalf of the group) unleashed his fury, complaining that one could expect such hostility from an antisemite, but from a Jew—what a bizarre novelty! Moreover, if a "learned" Jew made such claims, they were likely to gain credence among non-Jews. "Decide for yourselves, my dear sirs, is there room in your journal for accusations such as those lodged in that article? And if those of our people who have turned toward enlightenment attribute to us 'a moral and material fall, illicit trading and manipulations, cheating in weights and measurements, disorder in our homes, illnesses, the bad education of children, parasitism,' and if we add disgraceful poverty, with what then is left for our enemies to reproach us?"[16] The author ended by noting that Levanda has talent. Better it should serve knowledge and truth (nauka i istina).

For these readers. Levanda had gone too far. Many subscribers cancelled. They were not only offended, they were shocked by Rassvet. Unfamiliar with Jewish newspapers, they did not know how Maskilim express themselves. In fact, Levanda was not very different from other Maskilim, like the Hebrew writer Abraham Kovner, or the Russians Vissarion Belinsky and Nikolai Chernyshevsky. When Rassvet closed after only a year due in part to a lack of subscribers, Rabinovich regretted the loss of engagement with readers: "we openly

---

13   Ibid., 9.

14   "Vozrozhenie na stat'iu L. L. Iz Igumena, Zhelezograda i prochikh Minskikh podpischikov Rassveta," Rassvet, July 29, 1860, 154-156.

15   Ibid., 154.

16   Ibid.

interacted with a mass of people who in one or another way resembled us, sharing the same ambitions, harboring the same hopes."[17] One can presume that *Rassvet* had a diverse readership; some supported the radical Haskalah, while others did not.

When Levanda wrote another tough article, on elections for a rabbi in Minsk, he may have reconsidered the role of Russian Jewish journalist.[18] Prompted by the readers' letter (and *Rassvet*'s shaky financial condition), he considered balancing criticism with admiration for Jewish tradition. Perhaps this would appeal more to readers who were sensitive to criticism. Indeed, Osip Rabinovich promoted this approach.

In issue 22 of *Rassvet*, in an article entitled, "The Jewish Colony of Morgunovka," Levanda displayed a change of approach. Here he gushed with praise for Jewish life in the agricultural settlement. If everything in Minsk Province was bad, now everything in the Kherson Province in Ukraine was good. "You only need to visit the Jewish colony of Morgunovka," he wrote, "to be convinced how unfair is the accusation that our people are incapable of useful farm work. Jewish colonists here are seriously engaged in cultivating wheat for bread."[19] Levanda turned from attacker to defender. He rejected the accusation that Jews cannot make good farmers. Jews can excel at all kinds of productive labor, just as anyone else, he argued.

As if to distinguish the nefarious city Jew from the superior country Jew, Levanda underscored the virtue of modesty. He asks Morgunov, the colony's founder, why he hasn't yet received the title Distinguished Citizen. Morgunov explains that he requested the honor, he didn't lobby for it, and therefore he didn't get it.[20] Levanda has his own opinion. "The services of the founder are tremendous in this aspect. He showed himself to be an entirely meritorious person who loves his people not only in speech, but in action too, who fully understands the obligation of a true son of his fatherland."[21] Although only 250 individuals work in the colony, someday it might serve as a model for all of Russian Jewry.

---

17   Osip Rabinovich, "Vnutrennie izvestiia: Odessa," *Rassvet*, May 19, 1861, 827.

18   Lev Levanda, "Vybory ravvina v Minske," *Rassvet*, July 1, 1860, 87-91.

19   Lev Levanda, "Evreiskaia Koloniia Morgunovka, Khersonskoi gubernii, Bobrynetskogo uezda," *Rassvet*, October 2, 1860, 352-354.

20   Ibid., 354.

21   Ibid.

One would think Levanda's article satisfied the editor. Indeed, Rabinovich expressed his approval in a comment at the article's end. Since Levanda and Rabinovich knew each other well and could correspond privately, the commendation likely had another purpose. Rabinovich wanted readers to know that they wouldn't encounter more hostile criticism and thus should not cancel their subscriptions. "We extend our gratitude to the author for the pleasure that we got from his article," he wrote. "We are sure that all of *Rassvet*'s readers will share this pleasure. We would like to get further details about this amazing colony, the means and tools that the founder has used in order to entice city Jews to practice agriculture and learn this difficult skill; [we would like] further details about the quantity of land allotted to them, and the charges that are levied in this context, etc."[22]

Levanda pondered his experiences in an article "Awakening (Letter to the Editor)," which appeared in *Sion*'s first issue (July 4, 1861). Describing his struggle to find the right tone in *Rassvet*, he mused, "So if anyone were to ask me now 'what is the easiest thing in the world and what is the hardest?' instead of giving the classic answer I would answer as follows: 'The easiest thing–by which I mean the least burdensome or lightest thing–is eiderdown and the hardest thing is to be an employee or staff writer in any Jewish current affairs journal.'"[23] He complained that the smallest criticism is treated by the Jewish community as a full-scale attack. He poured out his sufferings—being accused of atheism, and worse. Why bother offering a positive picture, mentioning that they have a Talmud Torah school, a poor house, and a clinic? In fact, things are not really so wonderful. In fact, more and more people are awakening, seeing the truth, seeking change:

> It happened: suddenly someone awoke, rubbed his eyes and jumped up from the iron bed in the direction of the doors and windows to breath in the fresh air and relieve his chest; but alas! The doors and windows were sealed closed, no way out; suffocate with everyone else in the dark, crowded, stuffy and smoky hut. To go for a walk, the sleepless person makes a stir and whistles to one or another friend, but none answers. That means it is not yet time to awaken. He spits, the wretched, and then returns to sleep, detached from it all, until the awakening of every-one.[24]

---

22 Ibid.

23 Lev Levanda, "Probuzhdenie (Pis'mo v redaktsiiu)," *Sion*, July 4, 1861, 24.

24 Ibid., 26.

Levanda seems to be alluding to the enlightened individual who sees the coming new reality, but can't make change alone. He must wait until everyone awakens, however long that may take.

Although Levanda realized what readers wanted from him, he preferred the role of muckraker and radical critic. But as he noted, the world was changing. He was proud that more Jews "proclaimed themselves to be a tribe that does not live only by ancient ideas, but sympathizes with everything that 'deserves the sympathy of a person and citizen' and are unwilling to move backwards from the spirit of the age."[25]

Rassvet was essential, Levanda exclaims. It represented a new reality; it *was* the new reality. He continues:

> A year has passed since we have ceased to be voiceless block because we acquired language and publicly spoke out; we received a newspaper, by means of which we communicated to all who wanted to hear how we felt, what pleased us, what we cannot help but regret, and what awakened in our heart intense sympathy, and what we pass by with barely a murmur, entering far into the old school of suffering in which our people have a great deal of experience.[26]

Levanda posits a before-and-after; reality changed after *Rassvet* appeared, and it will never be the same.

Levanda's experience with *Rassvet* would be central to his whole career, and reflects many themes in the history of Jewish journalism in nineteenth-century Russia. They include internecine struggles within the Jewish community, conflicts among Maskilim, attitudes toward the Russian government, and government indifference. In Levanda, however, we see that the Haskalah was not only, or even mainly, a political program, but also served as a means of communication, a behavioral style, even an inner conscience. In this way, Levanda represents the total Maskil, an individual in search of self and a member of a group bent on sparking a social revolution among Jews.

Why Levanda swooned over *Rassvet* is an excellent question. As he frames it, Jews in Russia were fighting a war between ignorance and light, the old and the new. He acknowledged that he and his allies were armed; they had newspapers, their preferred weapon of engagement. The newspaper certainly offered

---

25   Ibid., 25.

26   Ibid.

a means of spreading the message to the masses, and it served as a power base to a new kind of elite, a Jewish intelligentsia coming into its own and challenging the Shtadlonim and rabbis for political power. Unlike their opponents, the Maskilim embraced openness to the non-Jewish world, and vied for power on those grounds. A new relationship between writers and the people developed out of this appeal to change. In fact, the democratic feature was essential, and the two-way relationship between writer and reader was actually effective. Levanda shaped his audience, and it shaped him.

It often happened that the Maskil, ideologically speaking, outpaced the community; sometimes, the two lost one another. This problem would plague Levanda throughout his career. He became less a representative of Russian Jewry and more a Cassandra figure who told an unpleasant truth ahead of its time.

Levanda in the 1870s: Proponent of Russification

The 1870s was a key decade for Levanda. It started with hope and ended with disappointment. Although reform in Russia fizzled after the suppression of the Polish Uprising of 1863, Levanda clung to his belief that Jews could find a positive role in the empire. During the early years of the reign of Alexander II, many Jews were convinced that the government would extend full equality to its Jewish population; something like the universal liberation of the serfs in 1861. In fact, events harbingered good tidings. In 1863, the government allowed some Jews the opportunity to live outside the Pale of Settlement in Russia proper, including Moscow and St. Petersburg. In 1865, Alexander II's government passed legislation to modernize army service. Previously Jewish recruits served twenty-five years, terms that began at age eighteen. Under Nicholas I, the government had enlisted children, "cantonists," for army service. Most, if not all, endured a cruel fate. Although the new reform required universal enlistment, terms of service were radically shortened; the average term was five years. Furthermore, shorter terms were made conditional on educational achievement in certain Russian schools. Finally, the government had implemented an incentive for Jewish Russification.

In 1867, the government finished its last reform for Jews, this one for the benefit of handicraft workers. It had been suggested that Jews had useful skills but couldn't make them available in other parts of Russia owing to their confinement in the Pale of Settlement (the fifteen provinces in the western region designated for Jewish habitation). This new legislation would allow qualified artisans to live in Russia proper and thus bring their skills to places that needed them.

However, for a variety of reasons related to proof of qualifications and the reluctance of Jewish communities to release a taxpaying member, few artisans could take advantage of this ruling. After 1867, reforms of any kind ended; the general liberation of Russia's Jews did not occur until the de facto abrogation of the Pale of Settlement in 1915 when Jewish refugees simply crossed over.

Levanda applauded the government's reforms, but as a radical Maskil he was never optimistic that the government would commit itself to change. Rather, just like his Russian models, Nikolai Chernyshevsky and Dmitry Pisarev, he placed his faith in the Russian people. Levanda envisioned Jews as part of the fabric of the Russian Empire, and aimed to show that Jews, often tagged as disloyal, were fully faithful to Russia and its people. As evidence, he cited the Jewish response to the Polish Uprising of 1863.

In 1871, he published his large novel *Seething Times* (*Goriachshe vremia*). Set in Vilna just before the uprising, it presents the choice facing Jews of Russia's Northwest Territories: to join the Poles, remain neutral, or support Russia. While Polish nobles pressured Jews to join the rebellion, the main character, a young Jewish intellectual named Arkady Sarin, argued against solidarity with them, claiming that the Poles had never fulfilled their promises. Instead, he proposed the Russification of the Jews. He bombastically proclaimed: "We have thought it over and have decided to turn to the right and link ourselves with Moscow. Instinct, fully considered, and finally the feelings of gratitude lead us there. We should never forget that barbaric Russia and not civilized Poland first began to worry about our education and development. We are obligated to Russia and not to Poland for the awakening of our self-consciousness." And he added: "We should not concern ourselves with which civilization is higher . . . For us the issue is not civilization, but about belonging to a people, i.e., about spirit and language. We live in Russia and therefore we must be Russians."[27] In the novel, Levanda raises the Polish theme. Why should Jews pledge allegiance to Russia? Jews are oppressed in various ways there. Nonetheless, he suggests, one should try to unite with the Russian people.

To his credit, Levanda displayed the disadvantages of siding with Russia. In one chapter, a Russian official sentences Sarin to two months in prison. Elsewhere, the narrator asks Sarin what he will do if the Russians reject the Jews, and Sarin answers that the Jews should prepare themselves for Russian

---

27   Lev Levanda, *Goriachee vremia: Roman iz poslednego pol'skogo vosstaniia* (St. Petersburg: A. E. Landau, 1875), 77.

citizenship. And yet Levanda exposes the Russian officials' hostility toward the Jews and their unfair treatment of them. When Poles denounce him to the Russian authorities, Sarin is jailed for criminal propaganda—that is, for advocating the Russification of the Jews. Sarin's offense, we learn, is related to his activity, not its message. It makes no difference that he supports the Russian effort; the fact that he acts at all is suspect. The dialogue between Sarin and the Russian official reveals Levanda's stark awareness of the distance between the government and the Jews of Russia:

> "Since when have kikes started to worry about their usefulness to Russia?"
>
> "Since the time when they stopped being kikes and started to feel like Russian citizens."
>
> "*Citoyens*?" the official became enraged. "There are no citizens in Russia, no *citoyens*, but there are subjects, do you understand? What did they imagine–citizens! Do we have a republic? We will beat that literature out of your head. We do not need citizens, we need faithful subjects, and whoever does not understand this, we will make him understand; that is why we are the administrators, in order to make people understand."[28]

With this conversation, Levanda outlines the conflict between Russian administrators and the Jewish intelligentsia. While the intelligentsia dreamed of emancipation, with the same rights of Jews in the West, the Russian government stubbornly withheld these rights. In reality, participation in politics, while not forbidden, held certain dangers for Jews regardless of which side they took. In the novel, Sarin's prison term does not destroy his faith in Russia, but the reader wonders whether Jews can ever make Russians love them. Sarin's experience demonstrates Levanda's uncertainty: Would Russia treat Jews any better than the antisemitic Poles had?

While he depicts Russians negatively, Levanda offers more a flattering portrait of the Poles. He has Sarin fall in love with the Polish aristocrat Julia Staszycka, the niece of Count Teczynski, the Polish rebel leader. Not only does she return his love, she is his equal in every way; not just physically beautiful, but morally courageous.[29] Having discovered a plot by the Polish underground to kill Sarin, whom the Poles believe to be a Russian agent, she tips him off. This might be interpreted as a betrayal of the Poles, but the author justifies it as a sac-

---

28 Ibid., 82.

29 See Freeze, "The Politics of Love in Lev Levanda's Turbulent Times," 187-202.

rifice for the sake of love. Here Levanda clearly departs from many novels of the period, in which unrequited love develops between a Pole and a Jew. According to Israel Bartal and Magdalena Opalski, this successful relationship is meant to symbolize the unity of the two peoples with regard to their cooperation during the uprising, despite their religious differences.[30] Nevertheless, Levanda reverses the schema. By having the Pole rather than the Jew sacrifice for love, he shows that a Jew, too, can inspire higher feelings.

By giving the Polish characters dramatic depth, Levanda elicits the reader's sympathy for them. Even the negative Polish figures are depicted vividly. These deep and humane descriptions can be contrasted with the portrait of Sarin, who comes across as little more than a mouthpiece for the author's propaganda. For example, one may contrast the depiction of Sarin with that of Stanislaw (Stas), a Polish rebel and a common murderer. In love with the Princess Jadwiga, Stas had earlier seduced Marcisa, who is now pregnant and threatening to inform the Russians about his participation in the Polish underground government. Sarin mechanically repeats programmatic lines, but Stas is revealed through his body language and his consciousness. We see his psychology, his inner self:

> With his head lowered and his hands folded across his chest, Stas began to pace back and forth across the room, while Prakseda [a well-known salon hostess], bending over her favorite instrument, strummed several rich cords and started playing a song and then the hymn "Boże, coś Polskę." Having finished the hymn, she rested a while, tuned her guitar, and again began to play again, but Stas continued to pace the room. His face was pale, disappointed. It was clear that he was thinking, considering some weighty thought. "So," he said to himself. "So . . . Still, how can that be? Impossible . . . Meaningless! Stupid! And such self-importance!" . . . A moment later, "And of course . . . it's better, than . . . After all, the Fatherland . . . the Count. . . . Jadwiga . . ."[31]

I am not the first to note the paradox that those characters who embody a pro-Russian ideology are poorly drawn in comparison with the Polish aristocrats. In his 1913 article on Levanda, the historian Julian Gessen contends that "Sarin is too schematic, but alongside him one finds in the novel living imag-

---

30   Magdalena Opalski and Israel Bartal, *Poles and Jews: A Failed Brotherhood* (Hanover, NH: Brandeis University Press, 1992), 96.

31   Levanda, *Goriachee Vremia*, 225.

es—for the most part from Polish society."[32] Although the novel is still a defense of Russification, we may wonder about Levanda's unconscious intentions. His depictions of individual Poles reflect sympathy for those characters. Furthermore, by having Sarin fall in love with Julia Staszycka, Levanda shifts the novel's message from "we Jews must become Russians" to other issues: love among enemies, the tragic fate of the Poles, and so forth.

Why did Levanda undermine the main ideological message of the novel? An examination of the historical background against which the novel was written can help answer this question. Although the plot unfolds during the Polish Uprising of 1863, the novel first appeared in 1871–73, in the first three issues of *Evreiskaia Biblioteka*, and was presumably written during this time. In the years before the novel's publication, Levanda served on the Vilna Commission, which was set up to elicit Jewish reactions to Jacob Brafman's plan to turn the Jewish masses from urban dwellers into peasants. The commission submitted its final report in 1870, and, according to John Klier, "With the governor-general's blessing, not only rejected plans to subordinate Jews to the peasant village administration, but also sent a recommendation to the central government that the Pale of Settlement be abolished, and Jews permitted to reside throughout the Russian Empire."[33] Unfortunately, in the late 1860s and early 1870s the central government shifted its position on Jewish reform from support to open hostility, and the Ministry of the Interior rejected the commission's proposals.

Emblematic of the change in policy was the government-financed publication of Jacob Brafman's anti-Jewish tract *The Book of the Kahal*, which went through four printings between 1867 and 1881. Brafman argued that the Jews had actually retained their Kahal (autonomous Jewish administration) despite the fact that it had been abolished by law in 1844. He claimed that Jews were bent on world domination. Foreshadowing tragic times to come, the government failed to help the victims of the Odessa pogrom of March 1871 or seriously pursue the culprits.

In this context, Levanda's contradictory treatment of Russification and Russian antisemitism is understandable. He still hoped for Jewish integration into Russia society, and gave Sarin the role of sermonizer, but he was not blind to

---

32 Iu. Gessen, "Lev Osipovich Levanda," *Evreiskaia entsiklopediia: Svod znanii o evreistve i ego kul'ture v proshlom i nastoiashchem*, 16 vols. (St. Petersburg: Brokgauz i Efron, 1907-1913), 10:61.

33 Klier, "Jew as Russifier," 38.

obstacles. Moreover, he had already displayed admiration for various Poles, and invoked the Polish theme to outline the deficiencies in the Russian treatment of Jews, as well as Polish shortcomings.

By the mid-1870s, the cultural atmosphere for educated Jews like Levanda began to shift. Levanda and other Jewish journalists perceived a change in the younger generation that was impatient for the material benefits of integration and cared little about questions of collective identity or respect. They only cared about themselves, said Jewish journalists, and Levanda also criticized the new selfish professionals. He mocked parents who, in seeking marriage for their daughters, would only consider a university graduate who could attain the right to live in a major Russian city.

Levanda portrayed such people in his novel *The Big Scam* (*Bol'shoi remiz*), which was written in the late 1870s, when capitalism was taking hold in Russia, and Jews were among the most energetic businessmen in the country.[34] Levanda condemned their swelling ambitions, fearing that their success would lead to increased antisemitism. In two of his other writings of the period "Our Domestic Affairs (Letter from the North-West Territories)" (1877) and the novel *Confessions of a Wheeler-Dealer* (1880),[35] Levanda criticized the new Jewish youth, who, indifferent to morality, religion, and tradition, and disloyal to other Jews, threw everything aside for the sake of private enrichment.

Levanda's criticism of capitalism in *The Big Scam* can be found in his treatment of the Jewish merchant who seeks to become rich by defrauding fellow Jews. The author offers a positive alternative in his depiction of the two young musicians, who set themselves worthwhile goals. Significantly, the key to their success hinges on the figure of the Polish teacher. The aristocratic Pole serves as a model for the two young Jews, who are encouraged to rid themselves of their provincial Jewish manners and become cultured. The Jews, however, use their newly attained cultivation to attain material gains rather than become the kind of aristocrat that Levanda clearly valorizes.

Strangely, the novel features no Russians. The Polish teacher fills the role of patron. Jewish artists, writers, and musicians needed the support of an aristocratic patron in order to succeed in Christian society; as, for example, in the

---

34 Lev Levanda, *Bol'shoi remiz: roman iz kommercheskoi zhizni evreev* (St. Petersburg: Tip. L. Bermana & G. Rabinovicha, 1881).

35 Lev Levanda, *Ispoved' Del'tsa: roman v 2–kh chastiakh* (St. Petersburg: Tuzov, 1880).

cases of Mark Antokolsky or Anton Rubenstein, who were both befriended and supported by Vladimir Stasov.

Levanda in the 1880s: Despair and Fury

During the pogroms of 1881-82, Levanda held up the Polish example as a mirror to reveal Russia's deficiencies. When violence against Jews broke out in Warsaw in 1881, he wrote an article in which he contrasted the pogroms in southern Russia with the recent pogrom in Poland. Although he was enraged by the violence in Russia (which the government defended as an expression of the people's wrath against exploitation by Jews), he was somewhat heartened by the condemnation of the violence in the Polish press. The Poles, he wrote, behaved "in knightly fashion, refusing to kick a man when he was down or to applaud bestial behavior."[36] One could live in such a society, he claimed. As for Russia, he wondered whether one could "live in a society whose chance leaders and self-proclaimed councilors, dressed in a triple armor of lies, deception and unbounded arrogance, overturn the most elementary rules of honor, conscience, justice and human community, taking this for a highly patriotic feat."[37] Levanda's conciliatory attitude toward Poland did not last long, however, for in Poland, just as in Russia, the Jews continued to be blamed for the violence directed against them.

The change in Levanda's attitude towards Poland after the pogroms of 1881-82 can be seen vividly in his shifting views of the writer Eliza Orzheszkowa, who was known as a liberal and sympathizer with the Jewish plight. Before the pogroms Levanda heralded Orzheszkowa's novel *Eli Makower*, as

> the first attempt in Polish literature to depict a Jewish character, Jewish daily life and the attitudes of Jews toward the peoples among whom they live, without the conventional prejudices of the Polish criticisms or contempt for the humiliated and oppressed person of the Jew, but seriously, objectively, and with a very noble aim. This goal is the reconciliation of the two peoples by means of common understanding and respect, the reconciliation of equals with one another not in the name of some archaic tendencies or illusions, but in the name of a more rational economic modus vivendi.

---

36 Lev Levanda, "Pis'mo iz provintsii," *Russkii Evrei,* January 15, 1882, 28.

37 Ibid.

Orzheszkowa's achievement was all the more startling, Levanda wrote in his introduction to his own translation of the last part of *Eli Makower*, because the conventional treatment of Jews in Polish literature was so stereotypical. Every Polish author, Levanda lamented, felt the need to include at least one Jew, either a moneylender, an estate manager, or a tavernkeeper. Even the great Mickiewicz could not resist inventing Jankiel, "whom he remembered suddenly in the last minute of his wildest leap onto his unbridled Pegasus who, it seems, had no head or legs, but only wings."[38] Levanda claims that Jankiel was merely an artistic inspiration, a symbol that never came alive as a full character. Orzheszkowa, however, was a happy exception.

Levanda's positive attitude toward Orzheszkowa evaporated after the publication in 1881 of her article "On Jews and the Jewish Question."[39] Although Levanda conceded that her proposal that Jews and Poles be forced to study together and ultimately intermarry was not objectionable in itself, he was angered at her accusation that educated Jews were responsible for the failure of Jewish integration. He could not help noticing a paradox: only a few decades earlier, when Jews had resisted integration, they were left untouched. As soon as they responded to the call to integrate, the violence began. This paradox revealed the real attitude of Christians toward Jews. But, writes Levanda, Jews should not be fooled by these accusations and threats:

> They are false threats aimed at scaring us off the common path [. . .] so that we will crawl back into the nooks and crannies from which we emerged when we became attracted to the rays of light that have shined upon us too. This only proves that the alarmists are hardly acquainted with the natural history of our tribe. It is a fact that we are made up in such a way that we can only move forward, not backward, and for their part it would be a great deal more sensible if they would reconcile themselves to the indisputable fact of the weakening tribal isolation and our acculturation to the civilized world, for they will not achieve their aims: we will not crawl back into our abandoned nooks and crannies no matter what you do, whether you attack us or not

In Levanda's view, Orzheszkowa revealed the same callousness as those who were openly hostile to the Jews. Although she encouraged tolerance, she refused

---

38   Published as a pamphlet in 1882—pp. 5-7.

39   Eliza Orzeszkowa, *O żydach i kwestyi żidowskiej* (Vilna: E. Orzeszkowa, 1882).

to countenance real Jewish equality; she called instead for further concessions from the Jews as a condition for their becoming full citizens.

Once the initial shock of the pogroms passed, Levanda reexamined his ideas and found them in need of revision. He began to express new views in the Russian-language press, using the pseudonym W.[40] In his earlier works, Levanda had often used sarcasm, irony, and *skaz* narrative (use of a voice other than the author himself), just as Russian authors did. But now in the 1880s, he used these tools not to affirm his affiliation with the Russian literary tradition, but to mock it. Instead of showing confidence in the attainment of the great nineteenth-century dream of progress—the triumph of reason over superstition, prejudice, and oppression—Levanda doubts. In fact, one observes a mind that is racked with pain. The titles of his articles in the 1880s give an indication of his mood: "Flying Thoughts of One Unable to Grasp It" ("Letuchie mysli nedoumevaiu-shchego"); "Modest Conversations about Last Year's Snow" ("Skromnye besedy o proshlogodnem snege"); "On the Subject of How a Mountain Gave Birth to a Mouse" ("O tom kak gora rodila mysh'); and "Convoluted Speeches" ("Bez-sviazye rechi").

He was especially agonized by the nefarious role of Russian literature in the persecution of Jews. Formerly his moral lodestar, Russian literature was now a tool of his enemies. It had been used to betray the ideals of universalism and ethical idealism. Simultaneously, Levanda turned his bile on the community of progressive writers who projected optimism. He recoiled at their frivolous attitude toward serious issues. He referred to their attitude as concern with "last year's snow," that consists of addressing

> those questions of life, those agonizing issues of the day, those core inter-ests of our tribe with which our special Jewish publications, our writers and poets, feuilleton writers and journalists, are animated and inspired, by which they live and breathe, in a word, the whole phalanx of optimis-tic dreamers who by habit still believe in the power of the "word." How naive! Apparently they cannot accept that it is now impossible to "burn the hearts of people with the word?," although every day they are shown the futility of their words and the resistance to fire in people's hearts. . . . And it's all because those in whose name and interests the fierce battle is

---

40   Shimon Markish, "Stoit li perechityvat' L'va Levandy?" *Vestnik Evreiskogo Universiteta v Moskve* 3, no. 10 (1995): 122-123. The pseudonym seems something of a mystery because it is unclear why he needed it. The censor ripped apart some of his articles and everyone knew the true identity of the author in any case.

waged, regard it all as "last year's snow," interesting only for statistics in the field of meteorology.[41]

Focusing on the line from Alexander Pushkin's poem "The Prophet"— "glagolom zhech' serdtsa liudei" [burning the hearts of people with the word]— Levanda condemned Jewish journalists (he was one of them). By mocking the poem that for Russians of his generation represented a sacred promise to help the underprivileged, Levanda committed blasphemy.[42] The Russian positivists of Levanda's generation that included Nikolai Chernyshevsky, Dmitry Pisarev, and even Ivan Turgenev, had expropriated aspects of the Pushkin myth to enhance their ideological authority.[43] By criticizing Pushkin and Russian society, Levanda indicated that the promise of social progress (as projected in the Pushkin poem) was a lie. The poem reflected Levanda's rage at Russian literature. Pushkin, who previously represented everything good, had also turned upside-down.

Levanda continued his assault on Russian literature by reinterpreting Nikolai Nekrasov's famous poem "Who Lives Well in Russia?" For Levanda's generation Nekrasov represented the idea of moral progress. Here Levanda purposefully distorts the poem, thereby reversing Nekrasov's reputation and possibly disowning the entire Russian literary tradition. In an article from June 1881, he quotes Nekrasov's poem, adding however his own subjective commentary at the end of each line.

> You are poor (in bread)
> You are rich (in drunken stupor)
> You are powerful (in appetite)
> You are powerless (in will)
> Mother Russia!

Levanda explained his purpose: "The commentary in the parentheses belongs to me, not Nekrasov."[44] He continued, "The arithmetic here is simple and clear:

---

41 W., "Mimakhodom, skromnye besedy o proshlogodnom snege," *Ezhenedel'naia khronika Voskhoda*, March 31, 1885, 871.

42 On the meaning of Puskin's "Prorok" in the 1870s, see Mikhail Alekseev, *Pushkin: sravnitel'no-istoricheskie issledovaniia* (Leningrad, Nauka, 1972), 258.

43 Brian Horowitz, *The Myth of A. S. Pushkin in Russia's Silver Age: M. O. Gershenzon-Pushinist* (Evanston, IL: Northwestern University Press, 1997), 75.

44 W., "Letuchie mysli nedoumevaiushchego," *Voskhod* 6 (June 1881): 70.

'Russia is poor' plus 'Each piece of food is accounted for.' Plus 'a trend of inhumane thoughts' equals 'grab the person next to you by the throat,' plus 'relieve him of his pocket.' There is nothing unclear in this formulation; it is the alphabet of contemporary social relations over which it's worthwhile to cry and as a result of which any honorable heart must pour out blood."[45]

Levanda turned to his favorite subjects, the Jewish youth and the Russian government.[46]

In an essay from March, 1882, Levanda satirically mimics the voice of a Russian official: "'Yes, Moshka, don't you argue with me, you won't befuddle me. I am your slave and that's all. A big thanks to [Jacob] Brafman that he finally opened our eyes to see your underground machinations . . . But things cannot continue this way: the tsar brought liberation to the peasants from us, and we will ask him to liberate us from you, yes.'"[47] In response, Levanda comments: "But why do we buy Brafman's Book [of the Kahal] to destroy it, instead of reading it in synagogues, from the Bima [stage] as commentary to the other 'Book,' [he means the Tanach] that also gives us an advantage over the Russians and all native and dispersed people all over the world. I truly cannot understand why."[48]

Most readers are likely aware of the joke that Jews should read the antisemitic press because it's more optimistic than reality. However, the stylistics of the article, with its address, "Da ty Moshka" (Hey you Moshka)—second-person familiar and a rude diminutive of Moses—reflects Levanda's impression of Brafman's influence not only on language, but also on the Russian mind. Incidentally, the name Moshka is a pun, both a diminutive of Moses and the Russian word for gnat.

In these and other essays written in the 1880s, Levanda repudiated his previous optimism. He had believed in the good nature of Russia, the promise of Jewish youth, the value of Jewish journalism, and, above all, Pushkn and Russian literature. When it became clear that his ideals were empty of promise, Levanda disowned them.

After the pogroms, he began to seek new ideological solutions to the problems of his day. For a brief moment he became enamored with Zionism, or more precisely, Hibbat Tsiyyon and its goal of developing a Jewish outpost in

---

45   Ibid., 71.

46   Lev Levanda, "Privislianskaia khronika," *Russkii Evrei*, November 30, 1881, 1909.

47   Lev Levanda, "Letuchie mysli nedoumevaiushchego," *Voskhod* 3 (March 1882): 29.

48   Ibid., 33.

Palestine. In 1884, his article "The Essence of the So-Called 'Palestine' Movement (A Letter to the Publishers)" appeared in the volume *Palestine: A Collection of Articles and Information about the Jewish Settlements in the Holy Land*, edited by Vasily Berman and Akim Flekser.[49]

Levanda hailed the successes of the fledgling movement that no one had expected would survive. The colonists, he wrote, had forged a new path, started something practical by settling in the land of Palestine. Levanda raved about a change in psychology, underscoring the difference between generations. Earlier, he wrote, Jewish intellectuals sought solutions in theory; they wondered, how to solve the "Jewish Question"? Their answer depended not only on ideas, but also on their audience, the ruling powers. Levanda acknowledged that he was one of those who focused on rights, privileges, and duties, on agreements with the ruling powers. Since these theories had brought few results, the new generation turned to praxis. Levanda asks, "Has the solution to the Jewish question progressed from the time of Haman to our present day?" He continues, "The thing is this, through bitter experience, I have become convinced that theory, useless theory, will not drive the Jewish Question out of the vicious circle where it got stuck at the very beginning of its appearance. Our national instinct whispers to us: 'Try to introduce practical action, basing it not on words, but actions from which one may expect results.'"[50]

Levanda was deeply impressed with the First Aliyah, but he envisioned a more ambitious colonization project. He admired Britain's strategy in the Middle East because, as he understood it, the British were able to enrich themselves *and* bring profit to the native people. Levanda imagined that others, such as Russia, could also do this. In this scenario, Jews too could play the role of intercessors, serve as agents on the ground, and help realize the goals of the colonial powers. Levanda envisioned a large colonial project:

> The railroad and sanitation projects of Kasalette (deceased) and the Duke of Sutherland and the tireless activities of Mr. Oliphant for Palestine's Jewish colonization clearly show that powerful practical people who know where crabs hide during winter consider the Palestine movement far from a chimera or utopia, but as something practical that promises a fine harvest; and it depends on the attitude of the Russian

---

49 Lev Levanda, "Sushchnost' tak nazyvaemogo 'palestinskogo' dvizheniia (pis'mo k izdateliam)," in *Palestina: sbornik statei i svedeniia o evreiskikh poseleniiakh na sv. Zemle* (St. Petersburg: N. A. Lebedev, 1884), 5-19.

50 Ibid., 8.

government or Russian society to this movement whether England or Russia will benefit from the results. The more sympathetic the attitude of Russia, the more its success will be assured, and that would be even the right thing since Russia provides the main contingent of immigrants as opposed to any other European power whose Jewish population does not suffer from being considered "superfluous" and, moreover, does not cause problems.[51]

Levanda early on realized the material advantages that the colonization of Palestine could mean for Europeans. Later, Herzl would come to similar conclusions, but Levanda already articulated his plan in 1884. Like Herzl he saw opportunities for the colonial powers to develop Palestine and this effort would benefit Russia's Jews. Additionally, like Herzl Levanda saw the need to transfer "superfluous" Jews to Eretz Israel and he understood that the poor would leave Europe, although the wealthy might remain. Levanda explains "That the 'superfluous' should be offered and, if possible, given relief on both sides with a soft exit from an extremely critical situation. In addition to that, we hope that no one will seriously object, even those Jews who for this or that reason do not count themselves as 'superfluous.'"[52]

In contrast to Leon Pinsker, however, who agreed, even if not enthusiastically, to lead the proto-Zionist enterprise and head Hibbat Tsiyyon, Levanda only tenuously attached himself to the movement.[53] In fact, before long, Levanda cut his ties to Hibbat Tsiyyon and returned to focus on Russia, justifying himself by appealing to the cultural achievements of Jewish diasporas. "In its essence Jewish national identity composes an exceptional phenomenon in history, so much so that, despite logic and the most convincing theories, a definite territory is perhaps more harmful than useful. Jewish national identity strengthened itself and became crystalized precisely at the time when the Jewish people's land had been taken away."[54] Although Levanda seemed to advocate something like

---

51 Ibid., 18. Laurence Oliphant (1829-1888) was a British citizen who promoted Jewish agricultural settlement. A search for the Duke of Sutherland and Mr. Kasalette did not reveal identities.

52 Levanda, "Sushchnost' tak nazyvaemogo 'palestinskogo' dvizheniia," 18.

53 Steven Zipperstein, "Representations of Leadership (and Failure) in Russian Zionism: Picturing Leon Pinsker," in *Essential Papers on Zionism*, ed. Jehuda Reinhartz and Anita Shapira (New York: New York University Press, 1996), 191-209.

54 W., *Nedel'naia Khronika Voskhoda* 38, 1885, 1023; quoted in Markish, "Stoit li perechytivat'...," 135.

"diasporism"—the view that the Jews have developed more effectively outside of Eretz Israel than in it—he did not focus on this idea for long. Its function appears mainly to draw his attention away from Palestinophilism. Something else mattered to him.

During the mid-1880s, the seeds of his nervous illness were growing. As a child, the folklore scholar Mortkhe Rivesman saw Levanda in Vilna. He wrote, "The patriotism of L. O. Levanda and many other Jewish 'Russophiles' declined significantly. One should presume that the break in his sermonizing about 'assimilation' with the Russian people who had become the anchor of autocracy shook his entire spiritual world. He even became a proto-Zionist and died from a painful spiritual ailment at age 53."[55]

Simon Dubnov describes meeting Levanda in 1886. Finding myself in Vilna, I considered it my duty to visit L. O. Levanda who was ill. I was warned about the writer's strangeness; during the last years he had locked himself in and avoided meeting people, but I wanted to see the author of *Sketches of the Past* and *Seething Times*, the bard of enlightenment and Russification who had turned into a proto-Zionist before my very eyes." Dubnov goes on to write, "The conversation was lifeless until I mentioned his articles "The Fates of Jews in Congress Poland," that had been published in *Voskhod*. [. . .] Here my partner became animate and bragged with a child's exclamation. 'Of course I was called upon to write such things because I know Polish literature well.' And then again a strange coldness wafted from the twisted figure of this man who was far from old (he was only 52) with his obviously disturbed soul. With a mournful feeling I left this living symbol of the extinguished torch of 'enlightenment,' and a bit more than a year later, I read in *Voskhod* about Levanda's death in a psychiatric hospital near Petersburg."[56]

Observers give us a good perspective, but the emotions that Levanda felt may be perceived from his own expression. He doubted, worried, and suffered. One can grasp his emotional condition by examining his response to the suggestion to celebrate his twenty-fifth anniversary as a writer. In this exchange of letters (we only have Levanda's letter to Alfred Landau, the editor of *Voskhod*, and Yehuda Leib Gordon, the Hebrew poet, we perceive Levanda's emotional

55   Mortkhe Rivesman, "Vospominaniia i vstrechi (1877-1915)," *Evreiskaia Letopis'* 3 (1924): 75.

56   Semyon Dubnov, *Kniga zhizni: vospominaniia i razmyshleniia. Materialy dlia istorii moego vremeni* (St. Petersburg: Peterburgskoe vostokovedenie, 1998), 145.

loneliness as well as his refusal to consider his literary work an achievement or service to the Jewish people. At the same time, we also learn about Levanda's thoughts on Russian Jewish literature.

The story unfolds this way: Landau wanted to recognize Levanda's career, which had aesthetic, political, and practical ramifications for Russian Jewry. According to Landau, Levanda had improved the lives of thousands of Jews who had learned Russian from reading him. On June 16, 1885, Levanda replied to Landau, refusing any honors. "I do not want it [a celebration] because it is not the time for anniversaries, because I am not in the mood for celebrations now, because if I don't care to recognize the fact that the Jewish public has been reading me for 25 years, they shouldn't cheer that I've been writing for them for 25 years, but, alas, without any use. I know more than anyone else about it, and therefore I do not acknowledge any services rendered on my part and did not correct anything through my writing. It's sad, but true, and the truth is more valuable to me than holy incense, especially undeserved."[57]

Levanda's remark about incense used in Eastern Orthodox churches symbolized his sentiment; although holy incense smells great, it dissipates quickly, and moreover, here the incense is undeserved and therefore meaningless. Additionally, Levanda took issue with the argument that the celebration would recognize his personal life rather than Levanda-the-writer. For his part, Levanda wanted the anniversary to pass without notice as it seemed inauthentic to him. Incidentally, Levanda detested Landau personally, which probably contributed to the former's hostility.

We get another articulation of Levanda's feelings from his response to Yehuda Leib Gordon (Yalag), the Hebrew poet and contributor to *Voskhod*, who tried to intervene on Landau's behalf. Gordon noted, for example, that he had allowed such an event to take place in his own honor three years earlier. Levanda responded by listing the differences between Hebrew and Russian Jewish literature and between Yalag and himself.

> If the idea about my anniversary had come from a small group of sympathetic intellectuals who devoutly promised to bring it to fruition, of course I would have nothing against it and would consider this fact quite flattering since there would be no room for suspicions of falsity, empty imitation, and so on. But when the idea has been taken out on the street for the wild celebration of the incoherent crowd that runs after the

---

57   Lev Levanda, "Pis'mo L. Levandy," *Nedel'naia khronika Voskhoda*, June 16, 1885, 660-661.

chariot of the victor and the clown in response to various impulses—
then I am against it and cannot help but protest because I consider it
something absurd and entirely disdainful to be faithful to the crowd, especially ours that understands and acknowledges nothing but material
success.[58]

Levanda sensed cynicism in Landau's desire to celebrate his literary career. The
desire for a party, it seemed to him, did not come from genuine aficionados, but
from the "incoherent crowd." Attempting to explain himself, he compared Russian Jewish literature and modern Hebrew.

> The example you [Yehuda Leib Gordon] brought about your anniversary
> does not at all weaken the reasons for my decision. The fact remains that
> there is a huge distance between your literary position and mine. First of
> all, Hebrew literature actually exists and is acknowledged by everyone; it
> has a past, present, and future. At different points on the globe there is an
> enormous body of passionate supporters, almost fanatics, even among
> non-Jews. In a word, it has a *readership* that, although it provides sparing
> [financial] support, is morally strong. And that is why giving honor to its
> luminaries is truly pleasing and natural. The honor that was extended to
> you belonged to one of the most lawful and salutary things in our com-
> munal life. Russian Jewish literature is something else completely. Let's
> forget that for the vast majority it is *terra incognita*; even many of our in-
> tellectuals consider it a chance phenomenon, transitory, not normal, and
> even lamentable. Many of our intellectuals, who, up to now have become
> drunk and delirious about Pisarev . . . and similar Russian poseurs, brag
> that they don't know a thing about Jewish journalists and novelists and
> do not care to know; they brag as though it [this viewpoint] was some-
> thing terribly progressive.[59]

Levanda raised several important issues, but primarily he evaluated Russian
Jewish literature. He admitted that few knew much about it and most of those
who did, actually rejected it. Jewish intellectuals regarded Jewish literature as
beneath them, while fawning over Russian. Their intellectual level was low, as
Levanda implied and as their idolization of Dimitry Pisarev showed. However,
since Russians have little interest in Russian Jewish literature and Jewish intellectuals shun it, there was no one who genuinely needed a celebration.

---

58   Lev Levanda to L. O. Gordon, *Perezhitoe* (1912): 332.

59   Lev Levanda to L. O. Gordon, *Perezhitoe* 4 (1912): 332.

Levanda also examined his purpose as a writer, concluding that he wrote "alas, without any use." That conclusion was somewhat difficult to understand. Jews, the vast majority of whom were Yiddish speakers, had rushed to learn Russian. By saying that his twenty-five years of writing had no purpose, he implied that integration in Russian culture was without purpose. Levanda's claim was obviously influenced by the pogroms that appeared to invalidate his literary activity. His dejection perhaps caused him to overestimate the importance of Hebrew literature. At this time the future of modern Hebrew was in doubt due to the absence of readers. Gordon wrote his famous poem "For Whom Do I Toil," predicting an imminent end to modern Hebrew literature.[60]

However, there had always been another way—full integration for Levanda himself—but he had rejected it, preferring the role of intercessor, albeit a literary one, for the Jewish people. Even before the outbreak of pogroms, Russians had raised the issue of Levanda's purpose in writing about Jewish subjects in the Russian language. In a series of letters written in 1880 with Mikhail Fedorovich De-Pulé (1822-85), a former editor of *Vilenskii Vestnik*, we get a broader picture of Levanda's conception of his writing. De-Pulé, a Russian official with whom Levanda had grown friendly over two decades of correspondence, believed that the creation of a separate Jewish literature in Russian did more harm than good, and he encouraged Levanda to join Russian literature. De-Pulé writes:

> I do not dispute that Russian Jews need writers who have mastered literary Russian, that an artistic depiction of Jewish life in this language is useful, even necessary. But let A. B. and C. do this job, but not people with tremendous talent. You, educated Jews, now reject Jewish national identity, that's terrific! But if you are Russians, then everything that is Russian cannot and should not be foreign to you, especially to Levanda. Of course there can be a Jewish literature in Odessa, Kovno, and Zhitomir, but it does not have the slightest value to us, to our literature. These closed local literatures, that you created, are even harmful to a certain degree; please do not take offense. They give support to feelings of exceptionality and alienation, and, while they facilitate the dissemination of the Russian language, they do not facilitate the unification of Jews and Russians. [. . .] No one is forcing you to stop describing Jewish life, no one is chasing you from Vilna, sending you to Moscow, offering to introduce you to Ivan Petrovich Kornikov, Koialovich, even Aksakov, Katkov. But in the 13 years since we parted, you have not even gone

---

60   Michael Stanislawski, *For Whom Do I Toil: Judah Leib Gordon and the Crisis of Russian Jewry* (New York and Oxford: Oxford University Press, 1988), 104.

to St. Petersburg once (although you have been abroad several times). This is not Oblomov behavior [laziness], but a tendency—a desire to preserve your snail-like literary position.[61]

De-Pulé was an understanding person, a Russian administrator from the 1860s in the mold of Nikolai Pirogov, a liberal, who realized that members of the national minorities had sensitive spots. He therefore would not force Levanda to meet with such conservative politicians as Kornikov, Aksakov, and Katkov, but he also expected more enthusiasm for his invitation that Jews integrate as equals into Russian culture. He conceived of Russia as an extension of St. Petersburg, a city characterized by multicultural and diverse peoples and ideas. De-Pulé writes: "Petersburg is a wonderful central ground for unification, the integration of all ethnicities, diversities, and unique groups in the empire. Journals, people, and groups would meet you, a talented, entirely open person. If you lived in Petersburg one month, perhaps two months each year, or at least once in two years, you could say that you really know Russian life from experience. Only then would you become our Levanda, not the one who has become alien to his own tribe."[62]

De-Pulé leveled serious charges. He accused Levanda of cultivating a false position as a writer who preferred "separation" and avoided interacting with Russia, and because of this attitude, was "alienated" from his own tribe. De-Pulé, a liberal intellectual who supported Jewish integration, perceived Russian Jewish literature as antithetical to the goal of progress and advancement of Jews. Since De-Pulé saw Levanda as a model for others, he criticized Levanda's "snail-like" position which implied intentional ignorance of Russia. For De-Pulé, Levanda's behavior didn't make sense and to a degree he was right: Levanda's exclusive use of the Russian language and his (former) admiration for Russian culture implied a literary politics of assimilation, the entire or nearly entire blending of Jews with the diverse (St. Petersburg) population in the Russian Empire.

De-Pulé did not understand that Levanda was ambivalent about such a goal. Regarding assimilation, Levanda explained in a private letter from 1885

61 B. L. Gol'dberg, *Levanda kak publitsist: po sluchaiu 40-letnego iubeleia vozniknoveniia russko-evreiskoi pechati* (Vilna: D i Kh. Ialovtser, 1900), 46. Ivan Kornikov (1811-1901), Mikhail Koialovich (1828-1891), Ivan Aksakov (1823-1886), and Mikhail Katkov (1818-1887) were well-known Russian conservative politicians and writers. Oblomov is the title and main character of the novel by Ivan Goncharev.

62 Ibid.

that Russification was not the same as assimilation. "As far as I recall, the word 'assimilation' does not appear in any of my works, neither in the fiction nor the journalism. This word and the meaning connected with it are completely new in our life and I am not responsible for it."[63] Levanda and De-Pulé had gaping differences over what they understood by Russification and the goals of integration. Levanda was loyal to liberal ideas from the 1860s in which the Jewish community would be defined not by ethnicity, but purely by religion, and individual Jews would be entitled to full citizenship. His position was analogous to liberal, enlightenment notions of Jewish identity in Western Europe. At the same time, however, Levanda disdained the European idea of liquidating Jewish communal institutions. He desired the preservation of the Jewish community (as it was understood in pre-1844 Russia), while at the same time envisioning Jews as a productive population within Russia.[64] In 1885 Levanda rejected full assimilation: "Why not say directly that the issue is nothing more or less than the elimination of Judaism as a fossilized culture three or four thousand years old and the Jews as a three- or four-thousand-year-old shriveled-up tribe?"[65]

In his response to De-Pulé, Levanda had no explanation other than to confess that he did not want to become a "Russian" writer, at least as De-Pulé understood it. He writes, "Your letter opened old wounds, for which, it seems, there is no medicine . . . On the one hand, my origins, education, and forty-year paralysis in a vicious circle from which I cannot get free—precisely because it is a vicious circle . . . Everything always turned out that I cannot consider breathing outside our ghetto. I don't have the strength to escape and I am not at that age anymore, I'm far beyond forty; it's not old age, but not youth either, too late to repair my unreformed being."[66] Despite the encouragement to join Russian literature, Levanda refused, preferring to remain loyal to his own vision, to habits, and a way of life that, admittedly, made more sense in the 1860s than in the 1880s.

---

63   Lev Levanda to Markus Kagan, quoted in Markish, "Stoit li perechytivat' . . .," 127.

64   Nicholas II officially dissolved the Jewish community in 1844, but because the government refused to permit full assimilation, many aspects of the community life and institutions remained intact.

65   Quoted in Markish, "Stoit li perechytivat' . . .," 134.

66   Quoted in I. Sosin, "Period krizisa: obshchestvennye techeniia v literature 80–kh godov," *Evreiskaia Starina* 1 (January 1910): 54.

The subtext here—one can reasonably speculate—touched on De-Pulé's insinuation that Levanda had a responsibility to integrate. If even he, the best writer among the Jews, refused to integrate properly, what could one expect among average people? In fact, after the pogroms, accusations flew about that the Jews themselves were guilty because they had not made sufficient effort to change and integrate?[67] Could Levanda have felt guilty? Could that guilt have been among the reasons why he repudiated his life's work and why he said that he had written for twenty-five years but "without any use?"

Levanda drew attention to his emotional condition in his fiction during this period. In 1887, one year before his death, he published the novella *Avraam Iezofovich*, in which he treats subject of the talented Jew in Eastern Europe and examines Jewish identity as well as antisemitism. Although he portrays a converso in the person of the protagonist, Avraam Iezofovich, Levanda himself did not convert or even consider it. Yet the problems of integration and the price to be paid for acceptance are central issues in the story.

Levanda situated his plot in Warsaw of the early sixteenth century, the heyday of Polish prosperity and might. The hero, Avraam Iezofovich, a young Jew, is invited to serve as the king's financial advisor. There is only one condition: Avraam must convert to Catholicism—which he does.

Everything seems to be going well for Avraam until the Jews of Cracow grow restless about the conversion. To change Avraam's mind, they send Moshe Halevi Landau, the chief rabbi of Cracow and previously Avraam's teacher. After the meeting, the story takes a psychological turn. Avraam comes to realize that he has forsaken a sacred treasure by denying Judaism and expresses a strong need to return to the religion of his fathers. Avraam decides to try living as a converso, that is, he will appear to everyone as a good Christian, but secretly will perform the Jewish rites in the privacy of his home. With Passover nearing, Avraam prepares his home for a large seder dinner. The Catholic clergy, who despise Avraam and are jealous of his success, decide to unmask him before the king. Discovering their plot in the hours before the king will arrive to inspect his home, which has been built far from the city's center on purpose, Avraam and his brothers remove all the signs of Jewish practice and therefore save him. However, the story ends with Avraam's resignation and journey to Germany where he can live openly as a Jew. Unfortunately, Avraam doesn't find peace there either,

---

67 See Semyon Dubnov, "Kakaia samoemansipatsiia nuzhna evreiam?" *Voskhod* 5 (May 1883): 219-230.

but dies apparently from a pained conscience. In a key passage Avraam recants his conversion:

> Ever since I betrayed the holy faith of our fathers, I have not had a peaceful minute. I do not sleep at night, my conscience troubles me, and I am not happy with my life. All the honors that have been showered upon me by the king gave me no satisfaction; they burn me and I am ready any minute to give up everything and run to the ends of the earth. One should remain in the religion of one's birth until one's final breath. In betraying my religion, I made a mistake for which I will repent till my grave. Satan meddled and clouded my reason. And therefore I have to correct what I mistakenly did in an unfortunate hour. otherwise it would be better not to live at all.[68]

While the story can certainly be read as a protest against the phenomenon of religious conversion from Judaism, which had grown in Russia of the 1880s, Levanda underscored the dilemma facing a Jew who sought integration in a time of repression. Forced to choose between assimilation and his religion, Avraam makes the fateful choice that leads to his death. At the same time, the image of Poland is ambiguous at best. While Levanda exonerates the king of antisemitism, he portrays the Catholic clergy as an evil force. Pressuring the king to make Avraam convert, the clergy persecutes the protagonist, seeking his downfall at every turn.

As an allegory of Levanda's own situation, the novella reiterated what we heard in the letter from Levanda to De-Pulé: Avraam cannot bear the break from Judaism and his fellow Jews, despite all the honors and wealth that a high position in the government brought him. If the story is an allegory—Avraam is a stand-in for the author—then we can extrapolate that Levanda was offered the chance to join Russian literature (which, for him, is an honor equal Avraam's in serving the king) at the cost of alienation from the Jewish community. Levanda didn't go through the pain of a return to Judaism—never having actually broken his ties—but he felt the antinomy. He understood that his literary success would be secured if he assimilated fully, as did his colleague, the Russian Jewish writer Grigorii Bagrov.[69] Clearly, the psychological

---

68 Lev Levanda, "Avraam Iezofovich: istoricheskaia povest' pervoi poloviny XVI-go veka," *Voskhod* 1-2 (January–February 1887): 48.

69 Grigorii Bogrov (1825-1885) was a Jewish writer who wrote in Russian. His most famous book is titled *Notes of a Russian Jew* [*Zapiski russogo evreiia*] (1873). Bogrov converted shortly before his death to marry a Christian woman.

dilemma that Avraam confronted was one that the author, Levanda himself, had experienced.[70]

* * *

An Amateur Performance, the novella translated in this volume, appeared serially in *Russkii Evrei* between 1881 and 1882, which was one of three Jewish newspapers in Russian that appeared at the time in St. Petersburg (*Voskhod* and *Rassvet* were the other two). It was the first time that three newspapers competed to provide news and literature for Jews in the Russian language, which gave the impression of a Jewish cultural explosion. Among the papers dedicated to the cultivation of Jewish culture, *Russkii Evrei* was considered the most nationalistic. Edited by Lev Kantor and Lazar Berman, the paper attracted such talented and patriotic authors as Buki-Ben-Yogli (pseudonym of Lev Katsenel'son) and Grigory Rabinovich.

Although published in 1881 and 1882, *An Amateur Performance* seems to belong to an earlier time, perhaps even Levanda's earliest period, since it treats his youth in the early 1850s. Levanda portrays his own coming-of-age story, his immaturity, and yet, despite all, his certainty about his future as a writer. These themes appear far from the topics that influenced him during and after the pogroms that took place presumably while he was writing.

Regarding the government schools, such as the one that Levanda describes in his story, it is important to mention that in the mid-1870s, he entered into a polemic with Mikhail Morgulis, the noted Odessan civic leader and historian, over how to understand the schools; what were the government's intentions and Jewish reactions.[71] Morgulis argued that the government Jewish schools were unpopular among Jews and repeated the story (now a legend) that Jews were hostile to the new state elementary schools when they were opened in 1844.[72] According to the legends, children threw rocks at Max Lilienthal who had been

---

70 It is likely that Levanda wrote his novel in response to Eliza Orzeszkowa's historical epic, *Meir Ezofowicz* (1878). See "A Jewish Russifier in Despair: Lev Levanda's Polish Question," in my book *Empire Jews: Jewish Nationalism and Acculturation in Nineteenth and Early Twentieth-Century Russia* (Bloomington: Slavica Publishers, 2009), 32-33.

71 Lev Levanda, "Po povodu stat'i M. G. Morgulisa (pis'mo k izdateliu *Evreiskoi Biblioteki*)," *Evreiskaia Biblioteka* 3 (March 1873): 365-376.

72 Mikhail Morgulis, *Voprosy evreiskoi zhizni: Sobranie statei* (St. Petersburg: Tip. Obshchestvennaia pol'za, 1906), 102.

hired by Count Uvarov to lead the effort to diminish resistance to study at these institutions.

In contrast, Levanda describes his own experience: he and his friends ran into the arms of these schools.

> We know only that we, the boys, giving lip service to fear of the schools in order to please our Melamdim and running after the doctor's [Lilienthal] carriage and throwing snowballs at him, wished him all the success in the world and with impatience awaited the schools as an innovation. True, we absolutely believed in the tortures that boys supposedly got used to in the school, especially as our attention was drawn to the blackboards and class chairs that we often saw in front of the government school were supposedly common instruments of inflicting pain. Nonetheless we somehow were entirely convinced that with our commitment and talents we would not give cause for punishment, that torture was not meant for us, and therefore . . . we were happy about the schools; for one thing they were something new and our Melamdim [teachers] were actual torturers. We feared them worse than the devil himself.[73]

Not only did Levanda insist that Jewish children look favorably upon the schools, he recalls the positive atmosphere created by the Minsk governor who defended the project. In fact, Levanda describes how Jews quickly overtook Christians in knowledge and were lauded for it. Furthermore, he describes how wealthy Jews were eager to place their children in the schools too. Nonetheless, Levanda recounts that the rich kids demanded to know if the boys were forced to kiss a cross at the school.[74]

In the same essay, Levanda relayed his own experiences as a student in a modern Jewish school that was run by David Lur'e, a pioneering Maskil. Levanda portrays Lur'e as a hero of enlightenment and he shares his feelings about the man's courageous fight against the opponents of secular learning among Minsk's Jews. "The whole time Lur'e struggled as one against a large army of fanatics, obscurantists and hypocrites, won brilliant victories, produced a shift in the perspectives of his neighbors, and left the field of conflict only when the goal for which he had fought was finally and irreversibly attained, when the government

---

73 Levanda, "Po povodu stat'i M. G. Morgulisa," 366.

74 Ibid., 367.

came to him not to provide aid, for which he had no need, but to take over in order to reap the gains of his rich harvest."[75]

In her study of the role of the rabbinical seminaries, Verena Dohrm claims that these schools gave birth to the modern Jewish intelligentsia and were therefore responsible for the emergence of a diverse and unique Russian Jewish culture.[76] The rabbinical seminaries provided a place in which those boys who, inclined to secular studies, could develop and therefore avoid becoming "half-intellectuals" of the generation before them—for example, men who had some familiarity with secular knowledge but no comprehensive education. Furthermore, the seminaries gave them the chance to meet one another, make future plans, and bring those plans to fruition. In a word, the Jewish future in Russia was invented in those schools, at least in part.

In *An Amateur Performance*, Levanda expresses irony with a tinge of humor regarding the rabbinical seminary, portraying its positive and negative aspects. On the positive side, he describes the academic achievements of a few students who can read (and mostly comprehend) the classics of German literature. Here one might mention the Haskalah's adoration for German literature and its foundational idea, *Bildung*, understood not as education exactly, but as the formation of a self, a person, and member of the civilized world. This highly inspirational concept is consecutively valorized and mocked as the author focuses on the boys' pillow fights, consumption of too many pretzels, and silly pranks. The atmosphere in the dorms recalls fraternity life. The description of the dandy, his clothes, and preparation for witty repartee, reflects a mid-nineteenth-century aesthetic of the rising bourgeoisie, although clearly such concerns would be banished from a genuine rabbinical seminary, such as the Volozhin yeshiva.

Despite its name, the Vilna Rabbinical Seminary did not prepare its students for lives as pious rabbis. This institution was one of two in the empire that offered a high school education for Jews and served as a springboard for additional education in Russian universities. Few if any students became rabbis because there were more profitable ways to use one's diploma; for example, in a bank or business in St. Petersburg or Moscow.

---

75 Ibid., 369.

76 Verena Dohrm, "The Rabbinical Schools as Institutions of Socialization in Tsarist Russia, 1847-1973," *Polin: Studies in Polish Jewry* 14 (2001): 83-104; "Das Rabbinerseminar in Wilna (1840-73): Geschichte der ersten staatlichen höheren Schule für Juden in Russischen Reich," *Jahrbücher für Osteuropäische Geschichte* 45 (1997): 379-400.

The portrait of the students in Vilna corresponds almost exactly to the image we have of the Zhitomir Rabbinical Seminary, its sister institution in Russia's south (Ukraine). In his memoir of the seminary in Zhitomir, Mikhail Morgulis emphasizes a mentoring practice; older scholars befriend younger ones, giving them books and lessons and spending free time with them.[77] In Morgulis's account, learning to dance was a primary concern of many students. In both Vilna and Zhitomir the local Orthodox Jewish community rebuked the school, although leaders muffled their criticism knowing that criticism of a government institution could be construed as an outright attack on the government.

The mirroring of the plot of a theater play in a novel occurs often in the history of literature, for example in *Mansfield Park*. The common theme involves art and the attitudes toward art of the leading characters in the story. Levanda uses the theme of the play to draw our attention to the boys' sensitivity to culture, despite their immaturity and lack of experience. This interest in theater among Russian Jews is itself a provocation as it dispels the widespread view that Jews lacked a sophisticated appreciation of art. The enthusiasm for the play can be contrasted with the classes, especially those after the reform of the school and its downgrading. Everything that occurs after the reform earns the author's condemnation. Levanda is clearly angry at the teachers, the administration, and the government for destroying a vibrant school.

More importantly, *An Amateur Performance* offers the reader a portrait of the narrator, who stands in for the author himself. He is a budding writer with potential. He's not brilliant, but he's not a dunce. He represents Levanda's conception of the Maskil: hardworking, cooperative, and well-meaning. Rather than being portrayed as revolutionaries (*apoikorim*), unbelievers, or apostates (*meshumonim*), they are awkward indolent simpletons. Preferring to play pranks on one another, they aren't torn up by ideology. But in their serious moments, the boys can display conscience. For example, they decide to put on a performance that honors art and honesty.

The author's perspective on the Haskalah can be detected in the story's end, in which the Polish theme again occurs. Once the illegal performance has been reported to the authorities, it reaches the educational inspector who is the narrator's mentor. The inspector is a Pole who teaches literature and has been giving the narrator private lessons. Additionally, the two have become close; the

---

77   Mikhail Morgulis, "Iz moikh vospominanii," *Voskhod* 7 (July 1895): 92.

narrator is a regular guest at the inspector's home, where he impresses his teacher by reciting Polish patriotic verse by heart.

Since the novella is short and focuses on the school, we do not get answers to the many questions that arise from the story and its genesis. Why did Levanda write about the beginning of his literary career in 1882, the year of pogroms? What does the tale say about the Russian government and its commitment to its Jewish population? Are we supposed to link 1882 with the early 1850s?

On the question of Polish literature, we are clearly meant to see it as an inspiration for the narrator—presumably Levanda himself—along with Goethe and German literature, and Vasily Chukovsky and Russian literature. However, at the story's end, the narrator explains the process of becoming a writer: burn all your writings. He burns the play and tells us that he burned many more in the process of becoming a writer. Since the reader knows Levanda's history up to 1882, they know that he did manage to create a few good books. The author was right to destroy his "amateur," that is, inferior, writings. The ending, then, may be interpreted as a comedy: no one is punished and the author gains experience in both writing and literary life. However, Russian authors are introduced to fear of punishment early on.

In light of Levanda's career, it's hard to exaggerate the importance of the government schools in his development. The Vilna Rabbinical Seminary gave him opportunities to explore world culture, while lessons with the Polish inspector provided him with knowledge of Polish literature. Vilna itself was a mecca for literature because it served as a cultural crossroads in which at least nearly half a dozen literary traditions converged. The Nobel Prize-winning poet Czesław Miłość has written about this, albeit in the twentieth century.[78]

The only despairing aspect of the ending is the replacement of the serious teachers with incompetent slackers. The school ceased to educate, and exists only as a symbol of the government's former intention. However, while Russian power is central to the story, it is not monochromatic. The political crackdown at the school echoes government abuse elsewhere—the antisemitism and suppression of freedom that characterized the end of Nicholas I's reign. However, politics is not the central theme, as Levanda has nothing to say about other edicts, such as higher army recruitment rates for Jews as punishment for nonpayment of taxes, the recruitment of children, the expulsion of Jews from the countryside,

---

78 Czesław Miłosc, *Native Realm: A Search for Self-Definition* (New York: Farrar, Straus and Giroux, 1968).

the expulsion of Jews from within fifty versts of the border, and the introduction of the candle and meat taxes. Compared with these persecutions, the purge of good faculty at the rabbinical seminary seems relatively insignificant.

Nevertheless, it's hard not to view Levanda's story through the lens of the Russification project to which his name was attached. He became famous after the publication of *Seething Times* as the spokesman for Jewish loyalty to Russia, but, as we have seen, he was tragically disappointed by the pogroms of 1881–82. Instead of promoting Jewish integration with a carrot, the government gave up on integration, using Jews as a scapegoat.

Levanda of course bore no guilt for the government's behavior; he too was a victim. But one could accuse him of leading people astray with his optimism. He hoped, and tried to convince others, that Russia would modernize in a way that would benefit Jews; and he wasn't alone. A whole generation of Jewish intellectuals had imbibed the idea that the government could be a partner and that Jewish integration made sense as part of the rational modernization of the country.

To return to the Polish question, it is hard not to see that Levanda had more respect for Polish than for Russian culture. He portrays the school inspector with great warmth. No one can compare with him, even the serious teachers in the first part of the story. But he appears as a central figure only at the very end. Why not give more space to him if he was so important in the writer's development? Polish clearly isn't at the heart of this story. If not politics, what is the center? The play? Trying his hand as a playwright?

An Amateur Performance depicts an incident at a government Jewish school in Russia, and, through it, a slice of Jewish life at a reactionary time in Russian history right before the onset of political reform. A place of education is turned into an educational farce. The older narrator and young writer learn that the path to genuine artistic creation will be long and difficult, despite everyone's praise for his play.

At the beginning of his literary career in the 1860s, Levanda got a drubbing from his readers because of his radicalism. Interestingly, at his career's end, his readers wanted to celebrate him, but he refused their attentions. Just as in *An Amateur Performance*, Levanda rejected all the accolades from the public in order to concentrate on the genuine "truth," at least as he understood it. He wanted no anniversary celebration because he felt that his life's work was a failure. Thus, he preferred to burn his career, just as his novella's protagonist burned his play, in the quest for an authentic success which always eluded him.

Levanda died deranged, a victim of broken dreams of Jewish integration in Russia and the role of a Jewish writer as the messenger.[79] There isn't any consolation; or, perhaps, there is one. Russia often spurned its Jewish lovers; many Jews experienced the same unrequited love that Levanda felt for Russia; not all went insane.

---

79 For his last months in a sanitorium see S. Kuzniaeva, "Dva pis'ma L. O. Levandy," *In Honour of Professor Victor Levin: Russian Philology and History* (Jerusalem: Hebrew University of Jerusalem, 1992), 384-391; Moshe Perlmann, "Levanda's Last Year," in *Salo Wittmayer Baron Jubilee Volume on the Occasion of his Eightieth Birthday*, 2 vols. (Jerusalem: American Academy for Jewish Research, 1974), 2:717-724; see also Saul Gintsburg, "Meine bagegenishen mit L. Levanda (a letzte erinerungen)," in *Vilne: a zemelbukh gevidmet der shtot Vilne* (New York: Workmen's Circle, 1935), 468-471.

תמונת הסופר ר' יהודא ליב לעוואנדא ז"ל .

Lev Levanda in middle age.
From the New York Public Library Collections.

An Amateur Performance

(Reminiscences of a Student in the 1850s)

Lev Osipovich Levanda
(1835-88)

I

Winter vacation . . . To tell the truth, for a rabbinical seminary a winter vacation made no sense, for you will agree, what connection can there be between Christian holidays and a Jewish educational institution, moreover, an almost religious one? But no doubt rules are rules: winter vacations were part of the schedule of *regular* educational institutions, and therefore they had to be observed by us too, in our special school. Later these holidays were eliminated for Jewish schools, but at the time of this story they stll existed.

We pupils in the rabbinical seminary had nothing against these holidays. On the contrary, we were very glad to have them, because they were not only enjoyable, but also useful. Useful in the sense of self-education, autodidacticism, of which there was a great need in that rabbinical school. And not only in rabbinical schools. Almost all our educational institutions from time immemorial and, it seems, right up to the present day have been set up in the same way. To put it more bluntly, the teaching staff is so bad that a pupil, no matter how diligent and anxious to learn, will take almost nothing from his classes but his cap and the bundle of books he came with, along with the few scraps of knowledge proffered from time to time. Apparently neither teachers nor pupils expect any heavier baggage; the teachers therefore spend class time covering whatever it is they want to cover—of late that just happens to be *development*, as if you could develop something that doesn't yet exist even in embryo. In short, they do anything but teach, instruct, or provide factual exposition of topics. And as for the students, they have nothing to study but the teachers themselves, their customs, habits, weaknesses, and oddities. Studying subjects is something they must do at home, with the help of tutors or by their own efforts and intelligence. It is like that now, and it was like that then, almost a quarter of a century ago. And therefore, the three weeks free of classes, in the middle of winter, with its long evenings, and its snow and frost—which do not greatly incline a person to enjoy leisure in the lap of northern nature—were for us a real godsend. During those weeks we did not rest, but worked energetically in the common plowland, each one in his own private furrow. Each one had his own work, his own blank spot, his own lacuna in one subject or another, and therefore each one sat in his corner and mended, darned, patched, ironed, and so forth.

But the greatest share of labor and time went to languages and literature, which we held in special esteem. Everyone inwardly recognized that literature was the essence of that intellectual development, that European spirit, which we were striving for with all our might. The exact sciences and the social sciences we regarded as secondary, auxiliary means for the attainment of the chief goal, which was embodied in literature, and we thought we were acting quite rationally and practically in bypassing the auxiliary means and making directly for the *goal*. That was taking the bull by the horns. This seemed to us simpler and pleasanter and more advantageous, in the sense of significantly saving time we did not want to waste *unproductively*. And since we had virtually no guidance, without much thought we jumped straight from anthologies into the very heart of European literatures and congratulated ourselves on our swift and *brilliant* success, attributing the latter to the extraordinary capacities exclusively inherent in our *race* . . . It is true that in these "very centers" we were somehow not at home and even felt quite awkward, since we didn't know how to orient ourselves in those beautiful, but dense woods, in that magnificent, but confusing labyrinth. But this unpleasant and even horrible feeling was mitigated by the recognition that in any case we were in the *center*, and there . . . we would somehow get along. Whether we understood *Faust*[1] or not, at least we were reading it; and for the time being that was enough, because there were tens of thousands of people who didn't even know of the existence of *Faust*, and we did.

And the meaning of Margarete's song, "*Meine Ruh' ist hin/Mein Herz ist schwer* . . .*" we understood that very, very well. Gretchen was pining for Dr. Faust and for some reason feeling pangs of conscience. So after all, from the great work of the greatest German poet we did understand something or other. For such young boys as we were this was by any measure a more than frivolous attainment. To read Goethe in the original was not something just anyone could do. For instance, even pupils in the upper classes of the Russian gymnasiums can't think of reading Goethe, because they can hardly puzzle out German, syllable by syllable. The word "Esel" they pronounce "Yezel." What a joke!

But for jumping into the centers of European literatures you at least needed an elementary acquaintance with the structure of the languages, and except for German, these languages were not taught in rabbinical schools, and even German was taught in the usual way, that is, badly. Our German teacher was as handsome as Adonis and as stupid as two fools combined. He kept us for years on end doing *Deklinationen* and *Konjugationen*, and it always happened that while we were busy with declensions we forgot the conjugations, and when we were sweating over the conjugations, the declensions were steamed out of us, all the way to *der, die, das*. He did not introduce us to the general structure of the language. All that we ever learned from him about that was a few German curse words and the valuable knowledge that when a German wants to treat a person with contempt, he addresses him not in the second, but in the third person, i.e., he calls him not *Du* or *Sie*, but *Er*. And even this bit of information we acquired quite by chance. It happened that among the upper class pupils there was a one from the Baltic provinces who knew this feature of the German language very well. And once the German teacher, sending that Baltic pupil to the blackboard, used the word "Er."

"Wer?" the Baltic pupil ignited like a match starting to rise from his seat.

"Nun, du, Esel," the German replied.

"Was?!" the hot-tempered Balt exclaimed, raising his voice, and jumped up from his seat, grinding his teeth.

"Ach, du, Lump!" And in less than a second he had his feet next to the blackboard and his hands around the collar of the teacher, who turned pale as a sheet . . . This grandiose scene was somehow kept quiet by the teacher himself, who had no desire to publicize it. But the truth will out, and we learned about the episode and consequently also learned that the innocent German word *Er* under certain circumstances acquires such a powerful meaning that no decent person can endure it with equanimity.

However, we could not limit ourselves to this and other peculiarities of the German language. For our "leap into the centers" we needed more general knowledge, and this knowledge we found in grammars and dictionaries, which during the whole time of the winter vacation became our best friends, tutors, and advisers. Everyone sweated in his own corner, one over German, another over French, a third over English, and a fourth even over Italian. None of us, it seems, was preparing to become an opera singer, but nevertheless, some of us considered it *essential* to study the language of Petrarch. Our work thus was vigorous: autodidacticism attained its greatest victories, and pronunciation, accent, their bloodiest defeats. French, English, and Italian words on our lips, corrupted by Yiddish, sounded like the bleating of lonely rams or the incomprehensible jabbering of savages. But after all we were not preparing ourselves for salon conversations, but for literature. Literature—of course, Western European literature—was our main watchword; it was the main watchword of the entire Jewish intelligentsia of Vilnius at that time. All the best Jewish young people of both sexes lived it and raved about it, both awake and asleep.

The foreground, the focus of the educational fever with which all the *best* among us, or those who for some reason considered themselves among the best, were afflicted, standing like an altar in the middle of a temple, was the romanticism of Schiller and Goethe, with all that aureole that surrounded it half a century ago. The works of these twin giants of the German genius were devoured eagerly, read and reread countless times, learned by heart, to the extent that there were few among us who could not recite long passages from *Faust*, *Hermann und Dorothea*, *Die Jungfrau von Orleans*, *Maria Stuart*, *Die Braut von Messina*, and other favorite dramas. As for the endless *Lied von der Glocke*, absolutely *everyone* knew it by heart, frequently even children who barely knew their ABCs. Conversations, if they were conducted in German, were also studded with quotations from Goethe and Schiller. No one seemed to be able to utter a simple word; everything had to have a "twist," a quotation, a line of verse, a grandiloquent phrase, with the result that a native German from real Germany would have been hard put to understand the subject—what was being talked about, what was being said. This gave naive people, i.e., the majority of that generation, a pretext for thinking that they, by God's grace, were better Germans than the Germans themselves. For this they congratulated themselves most heartily.

Around the first-class stars of German romanticism there also gleamed a pleiad of secondary and tertiary German writers, who also excited and dazzled the reverent crowd of seekers of enlightenment. Among these were Klopstock, Herder, Gessner, Wieland, Jean Paul, Spindler, and . . . Byron, and Bulwer-Lytton. Although the latter two were least of all Germans, willy-nilly they passed among us for Germans, since we read them in German translation. There were even some who found it pleasant to consider Shakespeare a German, on the grounds that we read him too in smooth German translations. About the genuine German, Heine, there were very dark rumors, and in general he was not much favored, because he was too *simple*! He wrote as he spoke and spoke as he thought, and he thought whatever God put in his head. There was no way of *studying* or *working* on him. Whatever he said, you could understand right away what he meant. What sort of a writer was that? Any literate person could write like that. Take, for example, his *Reisebilder*. Who couldn't write something like that? Whereas the not always elegant *Witze* of Saphir were more savored and much esteemed; they were also learned off by heart so that one could later show off in society with a witticism taken at random from the Viennese humorist. All this German romanticism, eccentric, disheveled, with a large dose of lunacy, quite alien to the sober Jewish mind, in some amazing way was intertwined and interlinked with the most thoroughgoing rationalism of the French encyclopedists, the cult of whom was also widely popular among the Jewish intelligentsia in Vilnius at that time.

In the morning Klopstock's *Der Messias*, Wieland's *Oberon*, or Gessner's cloyingly sweet idylls, which carry a person off into an unreal world of Menalcases, Alexises, Daphnes, and their *two goats*, as virtuous and sentimental as the shepherdesses of Arcadia, and in the evening, Voltaire, Rousseau, Montesquieu, and other forerunners of the goddess of reason. The former were excellent and the latter superb. And all this was not studied like *history*, but ingested like food, which nourished thousands of minds and hearts striving for something new, lofty, and gleaming . . . What a muddle inevitably resulted from this in our understanding, thoughts, feelings, and convictions is obvious. Each one of us thought of himself as deeply devout and even superstitiously freethinking, i.e. something like a straight fireplace poker, without the usual bend.

But this muddle in the town was useful to the *school*, in the sense that for the students it served as a stimulus for work, for self-instruction and self-development, protecting them from the limitations and one-sidedness of the class notebooks, bad textbooks, and bad teaching, i.e. from thorough ignorance. The seething intellectual activity of the *best* people in the town kept the work of the best pupils in the school at a suitable level. Between the former and the latter there existed in a certain sense a moral connection and a frequent interaction, diligently maintained by both sides. Thanks to this relationship, the school never suffered a shortage of books for reading, especially the works of European literatures, since almost all the private libraries, of which there were many in the town, were at any time fully accessible to the students. And therefore, before the beginning of the winter holidays, the students scattered all over town, collecting large reserves of intellectual fodder for the whole busy period, loading themselves with books of the most varied content, and they, these books, were passed from hand to hand and devoured with fantastic speed.

Once, however, something happened that put us in a position to feed the townspeople with *our* books and thus to repay favor with favor. This event occurred when a certain student, coming back from town, shouted through all the rooms, clapping his hands, "News, gentlemen! Great news!"

We all jumped up from our places and surrounded the shouter from all sides.

"What happened is this," he began, squealing and rubbing his hands with glee. "On Rudnitskaya Street, right opposite the Church of All Saints, there is a shop belonging to a herring-dealer named Meyer, but known as *Haser.*"

"Haser, ha, ha, ha!" the students roared with laughter, much amused by this strange name. "Does that mean his children must be called piglets?"

"Wait a minute, gentlemen," continued the student, waving his hands. "Let me finish, or else you won't hear the most interesting part. The point is not that this herring-merchant has such a significant and probably well-earned nickname, but that he recently brought from Riga three barrels . . ."

"Of herring?"

"No, not of herring, but of books."

"Books?"

"And very well chosen. And since this Haser knows as much about books as his four-legged namesake knows about oranges, he is selling these books by weight, ten kopecks a pound."

"Really?"

"Go and look for yourselves, you'll see that I'm not lying."

We sent two enterprising students to do preliminary reconnoitering.

"A treasure, a real treasure!" the envoys reported on their return. "Everything is there. German and French classics, philosophers and historians. Kant, Hegel, Mendelsohn, Rotteck, Niebuhr,—Nösselt, Miller. And so many translations! The Zend-Avesta is there, in a German translation."

"And all that is being sold by weight?"

"Ten kopecks a pound. But there is a lot of junk: books on cooking, agronomy, architecture etc."

We grabbed our caps to take flight for this newly discovered California.

"Gentlemen," a thoughtful and practical member of our company stopped us. "If we go like this we'll spoil the whole business. If we all descend on him all together, this Haser fellow will get the idea and raise his prices. What will we gain by that?"

Acknowledging that this student had the right idea, we agreed then and there to mine our newly discovered lode gradually, one by one, and observing various safeguards. This way we managed to haul off to our rooms several pounds of literary treasures, among which were some real collector's items, which would have been totally lost if it hadn't been for us, since this Haser had no idea of their value and was using them himself for wrapping paper and selling them to other shopkeepers for the same purpose.

For a long time the whole town made use of our books, many of which to this very day are preserved in the libraries of local Jewish literati.

II

The winter holidays were pleasant and useful not only for intellectual highfly-ers, but also for highflyers of another sort. Just as in every educational institu-tion, among the pupils in the rabbinical seminary there was a certain contingent of dandies, who aimed to be social lions, heroes of the parquet floor. Whether there were any parquet floors at the disposal of these future heroes I don't know, for the "salons" were of course unprepossessing and modest, as unprepossessing and modest as was the life even of well-to-do Jews at that time. But, as the say-ing goes, the proof of the pudding is in the eating. The chief adornments of the unresplendent salons were the resplendent Amalias, Rebeccas, or Annas toward whom were directed the dreams of these young men yearning for love—to be sure, only platonic love. Thanks to the prevailing sentimental-romantic atmo-sphere with its sweet-and-sour aroma, there could be no question of any other kind of love. No one aimed for any other sort of love, and both sides contented themselves with mute adoration, languorous glances cast secretly at the object of one's love, suppressed sighs, and in extraordinary cases and under excep-tional circumstances, cooing like doves. However, this in no way prevented the Amalias, Fredericas, and Berthas, though indoctrinated in the empyrean and by moonlight, from in due course marrying not romantics, but thoroughly down-to-earth merchants and becoming ultra-practical Jewish housewives, having nothing in common with idealism and sentimentalism.

"But do you remember *Turandot* and *Kabale und Liebe*?"[2] You might ask such a practical wife a year after her marriage.

The practical wife makes a contemptuous grimace and—keeps on dress-ing down her cook for not being economical enough with the potatoes or the marinated herring. But right up to the wedding Amalias' thoughts had been a thousand miles away from potatoes and herring. They had been fully focused on ideals, and the Amalias had made the most strenuous efforts to maintain the honor and glitter of their "salons."

And in these salons people spent their time gaily, but—what was most im-portant—with sentiment. Seated around a table covered with a tablecloth knit-ted by the hostess herself and in the light of an oil lamp that didn't always smoke and stink, the *ladies*, with great feeling and sometimes even with the hint of a voice, would sing "Die Sehnsucht," Hector's "Abchied," "Melancholie an Laura," "Die Kindesmörderin," and other touching romances of that sort. The *cavaliers*, sitting at a distance, would be overcome with delight and would sigh silently, straightening their ties or vests. Singing alternated with games of "questions and answers" or "forfeits." The former game was interesting in that the random answers sometimes hit the target and contained a secret thought or hidden feeling—in short, an avowal, though of course one that was not binding.

"Who is dearer than life for me?"

"The person to whom you address this question."

The young lady turns as red as a peony, and the young man lowers his eyes with suitable modesty.

"Whom would you like to meet tomorrow morning?"

"The woman of whom I dream both awake and asleep."

The young lady gives a refined, but deeply significant smile, and the young blade coughs and adjusts his necktie . . . and doesn't think of getting up from his place. Those following the game burst out laughing and applaud, and the players are embarrassed.

The game of forfeits provided an opportunity for showing off one's wit, resourcefulness, and cleverness, if you had such qualities, or to be shamed for your dullness, helplessness, and lack of adroitness if you didn't. But in both cases the players were very merry and laughed and jumped and acted like children.

There was sometimes dancing to the music of a piano, and then the joy and gaiety of the romantics reached its apogee. The "society" would break up long after midnight, repeating with a sigh Schiller's line:

Der Wahn ist kurz, die Reue—lang . . .

It is therefore no surprise that the "salons" exerted a very powerful attractive force on the school dandies, who devoted a lot of time to them. The dandies were convinced that the time they spent in these salons was not only pleasant, but also useful, since little by little they were familiarizing themselves with the behavior, manners and *bon ton* of high society. And you have to do the dandies justice, there was much truth in this. They at least were less uncouth and uncivilized than many of their fellows who did not frequent the salons and were thus deprived of the softening influence of female society. And therefore the dandies had some justification in regarding the "salons" as a kind of "school," not to be neglected.

And they certainly did not neglect this school. If in ordinary times they devoted many leisure hours to it, during the winter holidays they devoted to it absolutely all of them. For the dandies too it was the "busy season," which they treated seriously and conscientiously.

Beginning early in the morning they began their efforts, fuss, and preparations for their toilette. Despite the meager resources the dandies generally possessed—that most unattractive government-issue clothing and those shirts of the most unfashionable kind—despite these unenviable means, the dandies had to dress in such a way that their clothing smelt as little as possible of government wear, of uniforms, or of the *seminary*, which was not at all suitable for the *salon*. O, if you have never witnessed these preparations, you cannot have the remotest idea of the degree to which "necessity is the mother of invention." It was astonishing what the dandies managed to create out of those clumsy and modest overcoats, the single-breasted jackets which buttoned all the way up to one's mouth, the military-style neckties made of coarse fabric as well as other articles of awkward government-issue clothing! . . .

But at the hands of these resourceful dandies, gifted with lively imaginations, all this seemingly useless rubbish was transformed into fashionable cutaways, low-neck vests, colorful neckties of amazing kinds, and trousers with side-stripes, which had just then come into fashion.

They sweated over their work, using a great deal of thread, Dutch or colored paper, calico, India ink, and other supplies, but they got what they were after: they emerged dressed almost in the prevailing fashion of that time. Add to that their young, fresh, and healthy faces, sometimes very well shaped, and the aureole of young men who were being educated and prepared to do their part for the intellectual and moral renaissance of Israel,—and you will understand why they were welcome guests in the "salons" and in some places the object of the platonic dreams of some pretty young head with curly black or smooth chestnut hair and with eyes that were fiery, penetrating, or languid and melancholy.

When they had finished their *toilette*, the dandies set off for town to make their *calls*, each one heading for the particular salon which primarily lay upon his conscience. They did not set off empty-handed, but carried books, as a suitable pretext for making the call, so that the girl's parents would have no grounds for suspicion. But since they never so much as glanced at the books they chose to haul with them, they would collect bibliographical information about them in advance from knowledgeable fellow students, so as not to make fools of themselves before their future female readers.

"Do you know this book?" a dandy would ask, showing the book to a bibliophile.

"I do," the latter would reply.

"What is it about?"

"It would take too long to tell it all . . ."

"But just give me some idea, in a few words . . . What is it about?"

"Well, you see, it's about what Pushkin said,

The less we love a woman,
The more we are attractive to her!

"That's a pretty good take. And is it an interesting read?"

"It should be! The author is one of the best novelists in contemporary France."

"What's the hero's name?"

"Gaston d'Aubigny."

"The heroine's?"

"Mlle. de Froncour."

"Good! I'll drill it into my head: Gaston d'Aubigny and Mlle. de Troncour!"

"De Froncour, not de Troncour!"

"That doesn't matter. Well, how does it end? Do they die or get married?"

"Neither. He leaves for India, and she enters a convent."

"They're both fools."

"They're not fools at all. You see, it turns out that *she* is the illegitimate daughter of *his* father, so in fact they are brother and sister."

"You don't say! Why that must be really interesting!"

"I told you that the author is one of the best French novelists."

"And who is now the best?"

"Eugène Sue."

"I know, I know. *The Mysteries of Paris, The Eternal Jew, Martin the Foundling,* and *A Doctor's Memoirs.*

"*A Doctor's Memoirs* is by Alexandre Dumas, not by Sue.

"I thought it was by Sue."

"Look out, don't give yourself away, you'll embarrass yourself."

"Oh, don't worry, in matters like this I'm very careful. I've never yet come a cropper."

"Lucky you!"

After dinner, the dandies' preparations were of quite a different sort. After dinner you could often find them reading books, mostly poetry. More accurately, they didn't read these books, but only leafed through them, selecting and copying out pieces that were suitable for recitation or singing, such as "Over Ocean's Blue Waves," "Palm Branch of Palestine," "The Hussar,"[3] etc. The pieces they chose were then learned by heart with greater zeal and persistence than their school lessons, which was quite natural, since it was a question of "salons" where they had no intention of disgracing themselves. For a poorly learned lesson you get a "D," but for poor recitation in a "salon" you would get a bad reputation in the eyes of the Amalias and Berthas, which was much worse than a low grade. Sometimes you could see one or another of the dandies sitting deep in thought over a German book with the French title, *Galanthomme...*,[4] which was passed from hand to hand in the school. O, this was a precious book, interesting in the highest degree and useful, because it contained rules and advice concerning all possible circumstances of social life, all the way up to court etiquette. Although there was every reason to suppose that these seminary dandies, even under the most favorable circumstances, would not go any further than Jewish "salons," nevertheless, just in case, they even studied court etiquette from this book, because ... "you just never know" or "stranger things have happened," or "every good soldier counts on becoming a general." These were the favorite aphorisms of our dandies, who had very ardent imaginations, not infrequently reinforced by the apparently very well grounded supposition that you only had to undergo a tiny little conversion to Christianity, and then everything would go swimmingly ... Some of these dandies subsequently really did undergo a tiny little conversion to Christianity; however, they still did not make it as far as court stable-men, no doubt because of insufficient knowledge of how to behave with horses—unfortunately no such knowledge was to be found in *Galanthomme. Sehr fatal.* But the most remarkable thing was that the book *The Well-Mannered Person* was the property of the rowdiest fellow in the school, so that there remained not the least doubt that the positive rules set forth in the book he had turned into negative ones. They taught him how to behave in such a way as to become unbearable to his fellow students, who were exasperated by his uncouth coarseness. Once his comrades got so sick of his rules-in-reverse that they—the comrades, not the rules—ganged up and gave him such a thorough beating that he was taken to the hospital bloody and half alive. He recovered, but he was expelled from the school; but that book—from which he had deduced the life philosophy of a gallows bird—was left behind in the school, as a living proof that even very useful knowledge can become to the highest degree harmful and dangerous if interpreted and applied incorrectly, so that for certain types it is safer not to acquire such knowledge at all.

But the most remarkable thing of all was that this ruffian, who would not submit to any school discipline, when he found himself outside the walls of the school calmed down and subsequently became a respectable and educated man who remembered his quondam exploits as if they were a bad dream. Perhaps it was it the government-issue bread mixed with sand that spoiled him, since his basic nature was evidently unspoiled, or perhaps it was something else. It is enough that life itself, with its method of hands-on teaching, proved to be the best possible school for him. It straightened him out and did not permit him to become an out-and-out *mauvais sujet*. If he had stayed in school, that is undoubtedly what would have happened. Despite its dozen subjects of instruction the school paid so little attention to the task of education, and despite the huge staff of teachers there were so few real pedagogues, that once a student went a little astray, he could continue on that course without any hindrance. Under those circumstances he would be expelled but not reformed. However, let us return to our dandies.

When evening came, the dandies, even forgoing supper, would fly off on the wings of anticipation to the "salons"—to take practical lessons in society behavior and engage in exercises in platonic love. In a word they sought food for the mind and the heart. To be sure, many of them returned with their hearts not only not fed, but even painfully wounded, from which they quietly moaned and sighed and spent sleepless nights, turning from side to side. But these are the sufferings of Werther, and they constitute the very sweetness of life, at least in youth. And what a pleasure it is to tell about your sufferings, and always from the very beginning, to some confidant who will sympathize keenly in your affairs of the heart! . . . And every one of them had such a confidant, a confidant with whom one could whisper in a corner, to whom one could confide one's secrets, one's hopes and fears, and who, for his part, would soothe and console and give the best advice he was capable of. To the honor of the confidants it must be said that they not only did not laugh at their comrades' feelings, but treated them seriously, and even with a kind of awe, believing in principle that love is a sacred thing, which only a barbarian or a frivolous person would mock. Although they themselves were not yet acquainted with that feeling, they understood its serious significance in life, even understood it very well, for surely Goethe's *Die Leiden des jungen Werthers* and Rousseau's *La nouvelle Héloise* are more than mere verbal exercises.

The confidants, besides everything else, were useful and even essential to the dandies in one further respect: since pupils on state scholarships *absolutely* had to be within the walls of the school by nine o'clock in the evening, and the young men who were luxuriating in the salons naturally had no time to think of school rules, the confidants' duty was to do everything possible so that the authorities would not discover the absence of their comrades. And the confidants fulfilled this obligation, resorting for this purpose to the cleverest ruses, tricks, and subterfuges, not to mention bribing the guards to open the gates to their comrades, returning long after midnight from a *ball*. And the success of the confidants' maneuvers was enhanced still more because *all* the pupils helped them eagerly. The spirit of camaraderie was very impressively developed within the walls of the school, and every pupil abhorred treachery. One of the officials of the school, a Jesuit by training, tried to introduce spying at one point, but he did not succeed. No one wanted to be a spy, not even those pupils who were deficient both intellectually and morally. Subsequently, many years later, when the head of the institution was not a Jesuit, but some sort of vulgarian, espionage was established, but that was already a time when the rabbinical institution had been demoralized systematically and fundamentally with a particular goal in mind and was on a swift path to decline . . . That was a time when espionage, denunciations, bribery, forgeries, informing, and other splendid things celebrated their witches sabbath—all in order to demonstrate that of which someone, somewhere was demanding factual proof, and demanding it at any cost. There was demand, and so supply appeared. So simple and natural! . . .

III

But even the non-dandies who did not frequent the salons were also people of flesh, blood, and nerves; they too needed rest and diversion, especially in the evening after a day spent over grammar, dictionaries, and books.

But diversions created a very difficult obstacle—one which, for the most part, because of our complete helplessness, we could not surmount. What was there to divert ourselves with? No sports were organized in the school; our educators considered that a superfluous luxury. For our day-to-day supervisors there was only one obligation, to maintain order, though in fact there was nothing to maintain, because with such hard workers and bookworms as we were there was never any disorder.

So the supervisors had nothing to do but pace up and down in the duty room, loudly yawning and looking at the clock every minute to see if their watch was over. To come out into the common student living quarters, to organize some sort of games for the students or simply to have heart-to-heart talks with them—such an idea never entered their heads.

The students at times were simply dying of boredom and *Angst*, feeling an almost physical need for recreation.

"Gentlemen!" some student or other would shout so the whole dormitory could hear, with undisguised despair in his voice. "Let's think of something! If we keep going like this we will go crazy!"

"Let's sing some songs," someone proposes.

"All right, let's," many agree.

Those who could sing came out into the middle of the room, formed a nucleus of songsters and struck up a chorus: "Ach, wie wohl ist mir am Abend," or the student song "Grad' aus dem Wirthshaus komm ich heraus," or the Russian soldiers' song "We are heroes, sons of glory." The *audience* listens and is delighted, the boredom disappears from their faces; they applaud and cry *bis*. The singers bow with comic dignity; someone stands on his head and applauds with his feet; two others roll around the room like wheel; there is Homeric laughter and cries of bravo; the merriment becomes general.

But the repertory of songs is soon exhausted; the singers sit down to get their breath back; the previous gloom, depression, and boredom descend again; once again the question begins to circulate: What can we do now? Sometimes we would sit mulling over this question until the bell for bedtime began to jangle at us from the guard room. The supervisor on duty duly appears, accompanied by the guard on duty.

"Time for bed, gentlemen, to bed!" he orders us authoritatively, going from room to room. "Candles out! It's already ten o'clock. If the director should come, there will be trouble."

Reluctantly we head for bed, scowling and snorting as we do so.

But we're not sleepy. Our souls are not satisfied, they need nourishment.

"Hey, gentlemen!" someone cries in the dark from his bunk. "Can't someone tell us a fairytale?"

"Levy! Levy!" people start shouting from various bunks.

This Levy was a master at telling German folktales. He could relate them so smoothly, in almost the exact words of the text, and with intonations that always touched us to the bottom of our hearts.

"I don't want to, I won't do it, kill me if you like!" Levy begged off, wanting to play hard to get. We plead with him, but he remains adamant.

"Gentlemen, let's bombard the recalcitrant one!" someone commands.

From various bunks leather pillows start flying in the direction of Levy's bunk. But this has no effect on the recalcitrant one, because he hurls back the missiles that were fired at him.

"Well start a cannonade with our boots!" we threaten him, swearing that we will carry out this threat if he keeps on resisting.

This threat is effective. Levy gives in and begins to tell stories. To the even, lullaby-like sound of his fantastic tales we doze off, one after another, sleeping the sleep of innocent youths.

One evening, when we were sitting and again beating our brains out over the question of what to do and how to entertain ourselves, one of the students said, "You know what, gentlemen? Let's put on a show."

"A show?" we asked, looking at that student perplexedly. The proposal seemed very strange.

"Yes, a show, a theatrical performance," he answered with more assurance. "Why are you looking at me like that?"

"What do you mean?"

"Very simple, we'll just up and do it. The *gymnasium* students also put on plays for Christmas."

"That's the *gymnasium* students, but we are pupils in a religious institution. It is forbidden for us even to go to the theater, let alone put on shows ourselves. The authorities will find out, and there will be trouble."

"The authorities won't find out. We'll do it in secret. None of us will tell anybody, and we'll bribe the guards with vodka so that they'll keep quiet."

This project appealed to us both for its own sake and because we would have to carry it out in secret, with all sorts of precautions, which is also quite fun to do.

"But for a performance we need a stage," we said as we began to think of the details of the undertaking. "Where can we arrange a stage?"

"We'll make a stage in classroom VI," said the initiator of the scheme, who evidently had not come forward with his proposal on the spur of the moment, but after considerable preliminary thought. "That's a huge room, rectangular, with two entrances, suitable both for a stage and an auditorium. We'll sew a curtain out of sheets or blankets."

"Better out of sheets; blankets are heavy."

"All right, sheets," the initiator agreed. "Sheets will really be easier. And as for arranging for the curtain to rise and fall, leave that to me. I know very well how to do that. I've asked wallpaper-hangers and carpenters."

"Good for you!"—we praised him for his zeal.

"I've already taken measurements and figured out the dimensions," he went on, coughing and choking, flattered by his comrades' praise. "We need five sheets for width and three for length."

"Is it really only three?"

"Three will be more than enough. The curtain doesn't begin at the ceiling, but three feet below the cornice. The curtain will have a border of colored paper, dark blue, for example, the color of the ministry of Education; but the very middle of the curtain will be adorned with a picture of the muse."

"Where will we get a muse?"

"Isn't Kaplan drawing a muse right now?"

"But I'm drawing Cleo, the muse of history," remarked the student Kaplan, who was right there.

"What of it?" the irrepressible initiator replied. "For one evening she can pass for Melpomene or Terpsichore; she won't mind. After all, they are sisters, the little kiddies of Jupiter and Mnemosyne."

"Ha, ha, ha!" we roared at the joke. "Poor Jupiter! A father burdened with such an enormous family! Where will he find the money for the dowries of his nine overage maiden daughters?"

"And what do you think the Jewish 'Bridal Dowry Support' brotherhood is for?"[5] someone observed.

"Ha, ha, ha!"

We moved on to the selection of the play.

"Boris Godunov," some clever fellow proposed.

"Will you be the one to play Marina Mniszech or the Pretender?" several people fired at the clever one.

"No," someone defended him. "He will play *the people,* who remain silent."[6]

"A splendid role!"

"And moreover one of the easiest. All you have to do is keep your mouth shut."

"Well," the clever one joked back. "I'm a specialist at that. In math class the teacher can't get a word out of me."

We argued and debated and came to the conclusion that we should choose some sort of light vaudeville. But where were we to find such a thing?

Again much thought and cogitation, but without any result. We were downcast, faced with a seemingly insuperable obstacle, since neither in the school library nor among the books that circulated freely among us was there anything in the remotest degree like what we needed for our play.

"Listen, gentlemen, to what I am going to say!" one of us said after we had been sitting silent and thoughtful for a minute. "In any case we couldn't cope with a genuine theatrical play even if we had such a thing at our disposal. For a real theatrical performance you need scenery, costumes, and other properties. Where will we get them?"

"Yes, he is right," those who were listening said. "Where will we get them? We talk and we talk, but we didn't think of the main thing. What shall we do then? What's the answer?"

"Here's what we'll do," said the person who had first raised the question of the main thing. "*He* (pointing at me) will write us something dramatic, we will learn it off by rote and spew it out from the stage, from behind the sheets, and there's a theatrical performance for you."

"Sounds good, let's do it," many agreed. "Well, will you write it?" they had already turned to me.

"Some playwright you've found!" I answered, scowling and waving my hand dismissively.

"Maybe you're not a playwright, but you can knock off dialogues, monologues, and couplets. "You're our famous *orator* after all, ha, ha, ha!"

The story behind that was that one of our supervisors, who had only the education of a chancellery clerk, had no doubt that the words *writer* and *orator* were synonyms. He found the latter term more to his taste and often used it to designate me when he wanted to specify what it was that set me apart from the other students.

"Well, Mr. Orator, haven't you written some new verses?" he would ask me from time to time, for some reason taking an interest in my classroom exercises and sometimes copying them for himself in a notebook in the most magnificent calligraphic handwriting, of which he was more than a little proud. This was what my fellow students were alluding to when they jokingly called me an orator.

"Well, all right," I joked, seizing on my fellows' word. "As an *orator*, I will write you a speech, and you will *perform* it from behind the sheets."

"No," my comrades shouted back. "You won't put us off with jokes. You have to write something."

"And if I don't want to?"

"Then we'll beat you up."

"And if I can't do it?"

"If you want to, you'll be able to. God knows, it's not such a difficult task. We're not demanding a Shakespearean play from you. Write a dialogue between two or three characters and we'll be satisfied. And don't forget that to some degree the honor of our institution is at stake."

"What does the honor of our institution have to do with it?"

"It's that, as you know, the plays performed in *gymnasium* productions are written by students. So it would be a shame and disgrace if not a single one of us could whip together something like that. Your good friend Pod***tsky wrote a play, even two plays; how is it that you can't do the same? Does he know more than you do? If you really put your mind to it, you'll run circles around him."

Suddenly the affair took a very serious turn for me, since it touched not only the honor of the institution, but also my vanity. I had a long-standing rivalry with this friend of mine Pod***tsky, a *gymnasium* student. It was a very peaceful rivalry, conducted entirely via literary experiments. Our referee was another *gymnasium* student, Zai***tsky, a knowledgeable fellow and a very subtle critic. He gave us topics, and we would write and then present the results for his comment and judgment. Praise from him was more valuable and authoritative than praise from our teachers, who took an officious attitude toward such things. Almost always his verdict was that I had more talent and skills of argumentation, but my friend was more widely read and had a better command of language. A year earlier two plays by Pod***tsky had been performed on the gymnasium stage, a vaudeville in Russian called *Two Uhlans, Two Swindles*, and a pastoral in Polish verse called *Szara godzina* (Twilight), to the loud applause not only of the students, but of the teachers and their families. I attended that performance and was beside myself with joy, seeing the dazzling success of my pal, toward whom I felt not the slightest envy.

"Well, what did you think of it?" Pod***tsky asked, rushing up to me right after the performance, with make-up still on and in costume, since he had played the lead role in both plays.

"You scoundrel, Richard," I replied, ecstatically embracing and kissing my friend. "You dumbfounded me. I simply couldn't recognize you. And Zai***tsky says you haven't any talent! You have two talents in one—literary and theatrical!"

"Neither the one nor the other," Richard objected, taking off his wig and using it to fan his face, which was red and sweaty from the heat and from three hours of work on the boards. "I won't be either a writer or an actor. Most likely I'll be a good-for-nothing fop. As soon as I finish the gymnasium and enter the university, hit the bottle hard, become a drunkard and end up a piece of rubbish."

"Then don't party, don't hit the bottle!"

"Quite impossible," he said with comic seriousness and throwing up his hands. "You can't escape your destiny. As for you, you will never part with your books, and maybe, little by little, step by step, you'll actually get somewhere. In any case you won't end up a good-for-nothing, a fop, or a drunkard. That's for sure."

My friend, one must suppose, did not become either a writer or an actor, because I have never encountered his name in the press. Whether he became a drunkard I don't know, because I lost sight of him long ago. After he left for Moscow, it was as if he had dropped into the abyss . . .

Naturally, I wanted to test my strength in the dramatic genre, both to save the honor of our institution and at the same time to compete with my friend, who, in the judgment of our referee, Zai***tsky, prevailed not so much by talent as by style. So with pleasure I took on the assignment of my comrades, who were absolutely overjoyed that there would be a play and that a performance would take place.

While we were rubbing our hands with pleasure, anticipating our forthcoming entertainment—something that had never yet happened within the walls of our school—the evening bell sounded, and we went off to bed. We went to bed, but I didn't sleep the whole night, since my brain stayed busy, thinking through the task ahead of me, which, of course, I wanted to carry out with honor or at least without shame. The whole of my literary authority among my comrades was now at stake, since their high hopes rested on me . . .

IV

So I was left with a very difficult task, as you can imagine, one which was almost impossible. To say nothing of a plot—and plots are not to be found lying around in the street, especially by such an inexperienced fledgling as I was, one who had seen so little of the world—I also had to take account of the fact that in the first place we lacked any means of putting on a play of even minimal complexity, and in the second place, there could be no female roles, there being no one to play them, particularly in view of the religious prohibition "Let a man not garb himself in the clothing of a woman."[7] But what kind of song can there be without a pretty lass? What kind of intrigue without a heroine?

Let's suppose that in the play *she* only appears as a figure in the hero's imagination: the hero will only talk about her, will perhaps sigh and deliver sentimental soliloquies, exclaim "Ach!" and "Alas!" beat his breast, and even tear his hair. I could manage all that: it would be easy for me to pour into the hero's heart the most flaming, mad feelings, even to the point of having him choke to death on them. There was no reason to have pity on Zimering.

Zimering was the student I had destined as the performer of the chief role. He was an athlete, had a barrel chest, and could yell as loud as five cobblers together, and his fists were formidable, even very formidable. I think that once I . . . hmm, let's say that I "experienced their formidable qualities" on my own person and they did not disappoint, indeed rather painfully so. Of course, he would have no occasion to use his fists this time: I won't allow any fighting in my play.

Zimering's fists came to mind only because I thought of him as a fellow who had the capacities of physique and voice to deliver the most fiery tirades. But you can't build an intrigue and denouement on tirades alone; they wouldn't leave any impression.

How to capture the interest of *the public*?

The effort to answer this question kept me awake all night, since what scared me most of all was the prospect of boring my public. How could I capture their interest?

To my good fortune or that of my comrades, Apollo, to whom I had prayed all night, at last took pity on me. I had spent many hours in an agonizing effort to find a suitable plot and was ready to lapse into despair when my brain, which had ceased to function and badly needed rest, experienced a sudden flash: it was a theme, and such an appealing one that I was sure it would capture the interest of my public even without a love story. In great excitement from this precious discovery, I jumped out of my bunk and almost started dancing. Wishing as soon as possible to share with someone else this burst of joyous feelings which had suddenly engulfed my heart, I began waking up the fellows who slept near me in the dormitory.

"Who is it? What's happened?" those awakened asked angrily, in alarm.

"I've found a plot!"

"What?"

"I've found a plot!"

"What plot?"

"A plot for a play."

"May the devil take you and your plot. I want to sleep."

The devil didn't take me, but with my raptures temporarily cooled by my comrades' kind greetings, I got back in my bunk, wrapped myself up to the top of my head in my blanket, and slept so soundly, like a log, that in the morning the guard had to ring his bell for a long time right over my ear before he could wake me up.

When I opened my eyes, all the students were already up and dressed. The news of my plot had evidently already managed to spread all through the dormitory, so that one curious student after another galloped up to me to ask what it consisted of.

"For the time being it's a secret," I replied to the curious ones. "When I've written it down, I'll show it around, but even then not to everybody, but only to two or three people, because otherwise it won't make any impression if every-one knows all about it in advance.

Everyone found my argument convincing and stopped harassing me. When I had washed, dressed, said my prayers, and had breakfast, I sewed together a notebook and sat down to write. As soon as I sat down to write, I was sur-rounded by the tenderest attentions. People who were used to reading in a loud, singsong voice held their breath and read with their eyes only, conversed in a whisper, and walked on tiptoe. One student stood at the door so as not to let any outsider into the study hall. In a word, all possible measures were taken so that nothing could interfere with my creative work. And my creative powers were on the boil; my pen slid along the paper with feverish haste. I filled up page after page, not stopping for a minute, because the whole plan of the play had taken shape in my head down to the smallest detail. All I had to do was to put into words what was already so vividly alive in my mind—a purely mechanical task. And the more I gave myself up to the job and the more I wrote, the more furiously impatient I became to see transferred to paper the images that were so vivid in my imagination. Believing at that time in inspiration as something bestowed from on high, something that descends on a person only at times and not for long, I was afraid that the "sacred fire" in me might go out prematurely and that my "creation" thus might remain unfinished. Therefore I couldn't help hurrying, couldn't help striking the iron while it was hot. So I began to write in signs, hieroglyphs, abbreviations. The sweat poured off my forehead like hail, my heart was pounding, I heard noises in my head, my hands were shaking, but I didn't tear myself away from my work even for dinner, which would have de-prived me of a half hour of "precious time." Actually my comrades brought me dinner in the study hall, but I didn't touch it, because to slurp cabbage soup at these solemn moments of "sacred fulfillment" would have been blasphemy and sacrilege; and besides, I didn't feel hungry.

By evening the work had advanced so far that I began to consider it half finished, and I calmed down a bit. Selecting a "committee" of three of the best students whose judgment I could rely on, with indescribable anxiety and in a voice breaking from agitation, I began to read them my "creation." There was no one in the study hall except the "committee"; everyone else had been asked to leave the room so as not to interfere with our "important business."

My judges received the first three pages in deep and serious silence, with a severe expression on their faces and without saying a single word, which seemed to me a bad sign. But starting with the fourth page, on the face of first one judge, now another there began to appear an approving smile, which my heart greeted like the first rays of the sun, rising just for me. My reading got steadier, calmer, more even and intelligible, closer and closer almost to proper stage diction. I modified my voice and intonations in accordance with the content of the speeches and the course of the action and even guffawed naturally, not just pronouncing ha, ha ha! With this sensitized reading I rescued even those passages I myself considered very weak. On and on I went, and the approving smile no longer left the face of *a single one* of my judges; at times you could even hear laughter, which was an even surer guarantee of the success of my play, which had been cast in the comic mode.

"Bravo! Good going!" exclaimed my judges and burst into applause when I had finished the reading. "The play is terrific. How could you say that you couldn't do it? You should play the chief role yourself."

"No," I objected to the 'committee.' "I won't take any role myself."

"Why?"

"Because as you know, I am terribly shy and don't know how to talk on the stage."

"How come you aren't shy in front of us?"

"You fellows are one thing and the public is another. As soon as I come out onto a stage, I turn red as a lobster, feel embarrassed and timid, and nothing comes out, or what comes out makes the whole theater burst out laughing. I know myself too well. I know how to act, what to emphasize—all that I know and teach everyone how to do it, but to act myself is just like walking a tightrope."

"Then who will get the main role? It's not an easy one, and the whole play is based on it."

"Let's give it to Zimering," I proposed, placing great hopes on the physical strength of that healthy specimen.

"To that blockhead?" the entire committee protested in one voice, jumping up from their seats.

"Have you gone out of your mind? He wouldn't understand anything about that part, we'd have to spend a whole week interpreting it for him, and whether he can memorize it in two weeks is a big question. The part of a lackey with no lines to say—perhaps he could manage that; but the role of a student—no way."

"Then who is there to play the student?" I asked, wringing my hands and with despair in my voice, since I had poured my whole soul into that role, basing on it the whole interest of the play, its only hope of success.

"It seems to me," one of the judges said, "it seems to me that Rosenroth would do a good job in that part. He is our clown and a clever fellow."

This was a very opportune idea, and we all seized upon it as an anchor of salvation, surprised that we hadn't thought of it before. The student Rosenroth indeed seemed to fit the role in every way. Actually in our opinion he could have coped with any role at all, because his special talents were formidable. We always said that it was only by an inexplicable quirk of fate that he landed in a rabbinical seminary instead of a theatrical school.

"Call Rosenroth!" one of the judges ordered, opening the door of the study hall for a moment.

Rosenroth appeared.

"This is the way it is, Rosenroth," the oldest of the judges began in a serious and authoritative tone. "We've decided to assign you the chief role in the play."

"I am flattered, most flattered," said Rosenroth, with an affectedly humble and blissful expression on his face, bowing to the waist. "To my very grave I will not forget this beneficent benefaction . . . My wife and children will eternally pray . . ."

We dissolved in laughter. Before us stood the pathetic, living image of a poor official who has just received some favor; even his chin and cheeks were suddenly unshaven, bristly, and wrinkled, although Rosenroth's real face was clean, smooth, and white. The most experienced actor, even a better than average one, might well envy his mimicry. He could do anything at all with his face, his facial muscles were remarkably obedient to his commands, and by nature they were indeed very thin and supple. In Rosenroth the theater lost what might have been a really first-class actor.

"All right, don't play the clown, but listen!" the person who had informally assumed the role of chairman of our theatrical committee shouted at him severely. "Will you do it?"

"I won't refuse."

"And you'll do a good job?"

"I hope I won't make a fool of myself."

"So it's all arranged," said the chairman with aplomb.

"No, it's not finished," one of the members of the committee objected. "He should first give us a trial demonstration of his art."

"Fine, I can do that," Rosenroth said with a gay and free-and-easy air. "Give me the manuscript so I can see what it's all about."

I gave him the manuscript, first giving a short explanation of the essence of the plot and the importance of his role. For about ten minutes he read the text quietly, to himself, wrinkled his brow, stroked his chin, meditated, and made some experimental gestures—in a word, prepared himself. Then, with a loud grunt and assuming a pose, holding the manuscript at a distance, and looking at it with one eye, he began to declaim according to all the rules of art.

Even the very first sentences, uttered with well-marked pauses, mimicry, and gesticulation promised something unexpected, unexpected even by me, the author.

Actually it was more unexpected for me than for the other listeners, because I saw before me a completely new person, one almost unknown to me, who was more interesting, and a whole head taller than the person my imagination had created. On Rosenroth's lips every expression, every word acquired a more concrete and more profound meaning than I had ever suspected when I created them.

I began to feel that he was reading something alien, not written by me at all; I didn't recognize my own creation, which now seemed to me pathetic and weak by comparison with what I was now hearing. And I felt such pain and anguish in my heart that I was ready to cry from vexation and despair, feeling that I lacked the power to depict that character, that fine fellow of a student, who was now performing before me in such a vivid, free-and-easy, and engaging manner. I almost began to despise and hate my hero, who now seemed to me a rag and a milksop by comparison with this fine fellow, who was all life and vigor . . . This strange state of my mind, which did not recognize what it itself had created, was all the more natural because after working for twelve hours on end without getting up, creating swiftly and unconsciously, besides my nervous exhaustion I simply had not had time to become familiar with the image to which I myself had given birth. For that reason when he was brought to life so vividly and intelligently, he seemed to me alien, a stranger . . .

In the meantime Rosenroth went on and on, getting more and more into the role. But I no longer listened. Troubled by what was going on in front of me, I sank into thought, and Rosenroth's tirades reached my ears like a distant, muffled rumble in which you couldn't make out the words.

"Bravo! Bravissimo!" suddenly resounded almost right in my ear, stirring me out of my pensiveness. It was the committee voicing its approval of Rosenroth. "You're a real actor, you devil!"

"Quod erat demonstrandum," Rosenrath answered gaily, wiping his sweaty forehead. "Listen, brother," he said to me, "I think it would be good to include a few couplets to spice it up. I'll show you where they are needed."

"All right," I agreed. "Although I don't see any great need for them, I'll write some to suit you. But couplets have to be sung, and where will we get the music?"

"No problem," answered Rosenroth. "I'll take melodies from *The Lawyer under the Table*. All you have to do is make the meter of your verses fit the beat of these melodies."

I worked for two more days, correcting and revising where necessary; I wrote those couplets and the play was ready. I called it *The Would-Be Teacher*.

V

The title *The Would-Be Teacher* obviously designates a plot involving school life. And in truth the main characters in the play were indeed students in institutions of higher education preparing themselves to be educators of young people. To explain why I hit on this topic and not some other one I must go back a bit. This explanation will in addition cast some light on the situation, atmosphere, and attitudes in the institution in question.

A little more than a year before, in the fall, the news came from St. Petersburg that the minister of national education was coming to the Vilnius school district to inspect its educational institutions. As was to be expected, this news disconcerted everyone disposed to be disconcerted, i.e., the administration, the teachers, and the students. And as is usually the case under such circumstances, all these people were intensely interested, not so much in the fact that a high official would visit, as in the personality and spiritual qualities of that lofty personage, so as to determine how to make a positive impression on him. Information from the most dependable sources said that the minister was a serious person, religious, and . . . *Russian* to the marrow of his bones. This latter quality had for many people an ill-defined, elusive meaning, and it was therefore given various interpretations, one thing one day and another thing the next.

"He is no Uvarov,"[8] one of the teachers would say, when we asked him about the new minister.

"What? What do you mean by that?" we kept asking, dissatisfied with his laconic response. "He's not a lover of enlightenment?"[9]

The teacher makes a gesture of impatience, looks timidly around, goes to the door and opens it to make sure whether or not there is a pair of ears on the other side, and says in a tone both mysterious and sad, "In a word, he is no Uvarov; I can't say any more; you will see for yourselves."

Almost right away we got a foretaste of what we would see. We stopped learning any new course material and concentrated instead on reviewing what we had covered already—moreover not in all subjects, but only in Russian literature, Russian history, and mathematics, i.e., in precisely those subjects that the minister *loved*.

All other subjects were put aside, especially *German*, which we heard the minister couldn't stand, since it was the language of *heretics, Protestants, and rationalists*, i.e., philosophers. From this information we students concluded that the minister was a religious man, but intolerant, and suddenly understood our teachers' mysterious statement that he was no Uvarov . . . For a minister of "National Enlightenment" this trait did not seem to us quite appropriate. We now understood the sadness of our teachers, and we ourselves began to feel sad. It is important to realize that at that time teachers, those menial laborers of the teaching profession, who were kept on short rations, were thoroughly imbued with the idea that they were serving, and had a duty to serve the cause of "enlightenment." This high calling lay upon them and on nobody else, and they took great pride in their mission. After the system changed, they continued as before to carry out the orders and plans of the authorities, but they did not approve of them or consider them the height of wisdom. They did not deceive either themselves, or others, or even their pupils; they did not lie without twinge of conscience; in short, they only submitted to the inevitable, but they did not exult in or applaud the new, obscurantist regime, but only lamented and grieved. And it must also be said that those who stood *over* the menial laborers of the teaching profession did not demoralize the latter, did not buy them off, did not try to benumb their consciences with luscious handouts. One cannot help giving great credit for this to the new regime, which did its business in the open, without recruiting "Swiss mercenaries" always ready to serve whoever paid best and without draining the public treasury, i.e. the people's labor, on experiments which have nothing to do with public education, which is the daily bread of any well-ordered society. This shows that the "regime" believed firmly in itself, was convinced of its feasibility and inexorability, and therefore did not consider it necessary to gain its triumph by artificial means. Let us suppose it was mistaken in its purposes, but its mistake was at least an honest one; and therefore much will be forgiven it because its *belief* was strong . . . Which cannot be said of another, similar regime, closer to us in time, which evidently had such a firm belief . . . in its own bankruptcy that from the very beginning it deemed it necessary to open people's hearts with a golden key in order to instill in them principles which it knew—possibly better than anyone else—were hopeless. This was the basis of the whole degeneracy of that regime, which aroused the indignation of everyone who had no direct interest in its triumph . . . But let us return to our story.

There began intensified efforts to memorize the wooden Ustryalov,[10] odes by Lomonosov and Derzhavin and other religious or patriotic poems so that we could appear before our lofty visitor fully armed with profoundly devout and loyal feelings, which were in great demand at that time in the higher spheres. We worked with great diligence, hoping to impress, since we foresaw that the impression the minister received would determine the further fate of our institution, which had been founded as an experiment and continued to exist on that basis. Consequently, this visit from on high, the first one since the founding of our school, was of the highest importance for us, which we did not forget for a moment even as we crammed our heads full of the most ultra-patriotic odes.

In relation to one of these odes, namely Lomonosov's *In Imitation of the Book of Job*, there occurred an episode which obliged us willy-nilly to expunge it from our repertory.

As it happened there was one student in our class who had been given the nickname "Vielfrass" because of his amazing gluttony. Wherever he was and whatever he was doing, at all times, day and night, he was always eating something. For this reason he always had his pockets filled with a goodly supply of rolls, biscuits, pretzels, and other such edible items. He had a box with two locks also stuffed with fodder, consisting mostly of raw carrots, rutabagas, pickles, smoked fish, rotten apples, and other such splendid provisions, which spread around them a particular smell, for which we frequently gave the glutton beatings, but without result. One day at our insistence he would clean out the box with all the stinking rubbish, and the next day he would again fill it with the same stuff. Even when we were about to go to sleep, he would be lying on his bunk under his blanket and still his jaws were working, stuffing his face for the coming night.

Once, when we were sitting in the classroom and reciting poems while we waited for the teacher, our glutton, holding a roll in one hand and the book in the other, chanted as he memorized:

> O Thou, who in thy sorrow vainly
> Murmurest against the Lord!

He recited and chewed, chewed and recited. We paid no attention, because we were used to this method he had of preparing his lessons. But it had to happen that just at that time the already mentioned Rosenroth, jokester and comedian, was passing by our classroom, whose door into the corridor was open. Standing for a moment on the threshold, he flew into the classroom like a bomb, ran up to the glutton, who was sitting on the windowsill, and shouted right into his ear:

> *O Thou who chewest rolls all daily*
> *Vilest glutton food dost hoard!*

He then grabbed the roll from his hand and—took to his heels. The glutton jumped down and froze.

All this was done so artfully, so quickly, and so comically that we simply roared with laughter. When we looked at the paralyzed figure of our comrade, ridiculous in the highest degree, standing with a frightened face and open mouth, not saying a word, our laughter reached such Homeric proportions that a "censor" came from the next room to order us not to make so much noise or else he would report us to the senior supervisor, who had charge of the conduct sheets.

The teacher of literature entered. Pacing up and down the classroom for five minutes, as was his wont, he nodded to me with his long, thin, and pointed nose, which meant that I was to stand up and "recite" the lesson. I stood up and began to button all my buttons, straighten my tie, put my hair in order, in short, smarten myself up. I did this because the comic scene that had just taken place was still vividly before my eyes, and was afraid that I might erupt in laughter. I therefore stalled my recitation on purpose. I also tried to recall some sad and terrible scenes and any unpleasant circumstances of my own, so as to put myself in a melancholy and serious mood. But when it was impossible to stall any longer, I gave a loud cough, fixed my eyes on the ceiling, and began:

> *O Thou . . . hee, hee, hee!*

The teacher stopped pacing and gave me a menacing, uncomprehending look. I blushed to the roots of my hair, began to bite my lips, and couldn't go on. Laughter gripped my chest and throat. My comrades, lowering their heads and covering their mouths with their hands, giggled quietly.

"What's the matter with you?" the teacher shouted at me, getting angry. "Recite the lesson!"

I turned even redder, angry at myself. I felt like falling through the floor. I couldn't look at the teacher and clenched my teeth, since laughter was still tearing me apart more and more.

"Stand in the corner!" the teacher ordered.

I set off for the corner with pleasure, supposing that the punishment would turn my merriment into sorrow and humility, and I would have no further urge to laugh. How wrong I was! Glancing from my corner at the faces of my comrades, which were strained to the last degree with suppressed laughter, and at the stupid, serious visage of the fellow responsible for our hilarity, I had to make a superhuman effort not to burst into full-throated guffaws behind the teacher's back.

"Next!" ordered the teacher.

The next victim stood up, began to cough and clear his throat and after a snort began in a voice not his own:

O Thou, who in thy sorrow . . . hee, hee, hee!

The entire class, no longer able to restrain themselves, erupted in loud, sonorous, Homeric laughter. I too roared from my corner.

The teacher stood in the middle of the room with clenched teeth and fists, now turning red with anger and now pale with fright, casting at us swift, uncomprehending, and scared looks.

"Tell me at last what is the matter with you?" he shouted, grinding his teeth and shaking his fists. "Have you gone crazy? Have you lost your minds? I will call the guards!"

One of the students stood up and began to tell the story of what had happened. The teacher calmed down and listened. As the storyteller progressed in his tale about the habits of our gluttonous comrade, the teacher's face began to relax, and a smile even appeared on it. When the storyteller came out from his desk and started acting out the scene of the purloined roll, the teacher, no matter how hard he tried, could not restrain himself and also roared with laughter, loudly and with abandon.

"There's nothing for it," he said at last, taking a pinch of snuff. "We will have to drop that ode, or else it might happen that you'll burst out laughing in front of the minister. If that occurs, there won't be laughing for any of us . . . Therefore," he went on seriously and decisively, "instead of In Imitation of Job let's take Zhukovsky's A Bard in the Camp of Russian Warriors. Go back to your place," he continued, remembering that I had been under arrest.

I went back to my desk, very pleased that the bombastic ode had been replaced by a more effective and reasonable poem.

VI

The minister at last arrived. We immediately felt his presence within the walls of our town because they started feeding those of us on government support according to the "Prescribed Menu," a copy of which hung in the dining room, framed and under glass, and not according to the discretion of the food concessionaire. There was a big difference. All sorts of things were listed on those prescribed menus. Just reading them made you lick your lips, especially on an empty stomach. And how inventive the concessionaire had been at toning down what seemed to him its too explicit phraseology! Finding too great a divergence between word and deed and standing on our rights, we sometimes lost our patience and carried out dining-room "rebellions," stormed the pantry and bombarded the head cook, his wife, and all the kitchen help with grenades made of rolled up pieces of meat, which gave off the smell of fried carrion. But our rebellions ended the same way as rebellions of the weak against the strong always end.

We were subdued and judged according to categories: *instigators* were sent to the punishment cell on bread and water; *co-conspirators* had conduct points docked; *active participants* were given reprimands and warned in the future not to let themselves be drawn into the criminal activities of *subversives*. But with the arrival of the minister the "Prescribed Menu" suddenly ceased to be a dead letter, and for the first time we got up from the table feeling sufficiently sated. We even stopped stealing bread from the baskets to assuage our after-dinner hunger with what was an unusual dessert, one probably not to be found in any cookbook, not even one written for the Tungus people. Besides that, on our bunks some good-quality, warm, soft woolen blankets suddenly appeared out of nowhere, only to disappear to the same destination soon afterwards. And on the director's face deep wrinkles appeared and also a specific expression, something like that of a wild animal when it is either frightened or enraged. He spent hours and hours pacing up and down the courtyard with slow, but firm steps, with his head lowered, casting vicious looks from side to side and biting his utterly bloodless lips. From time to time he would stop in front of first the well, now the outhouses, now some empty corner of the schoolyard, and plunge into deep meditation, which usually lasted a full quarter of an hour. No one dared approach him at such times, not even the teachers and supervisors, who, indeed, were also scared to death.

The only person not frightened was the chief clerk, a real champion bribe-taker, forger, and rascal. Boldly and quite at his ease he went up to the director now with news, now with bound ledgers from which he read him something and whispered in his ear, to which the director nodded without saying a word.

As for us, in our student discussions, which were held behind closed doors and with lowered voices, we decided that the impending inspection was not a very pleasant prospect for our guardian. Why? Because . . . evidently his hands were not clean. That is what it looked like, we supposed. But that such an old hand, such a subtle Jesuit should so lose his head! That's what we couldn't understand, the more so since his right-hand man, the head clerk, was a master at the art of . . . erasure. Or perhaps he knew or foresaw that he was not to reign over us much longer? We both wanted that and didn't want it. We wanted it because we were sick of his style of educating us by officially prescribed hunger, cold, and other deprivations, which we had to make good with our own meager means. We didn't want it because in essence we respected him deeply; we were in awe of his satanic mind, his considerable erudition, his oratorical talent, his unusual tact in dealing with subordinates and students and his ability to give our whole school the appearance and atmosphere of an institution of higher education, which elevated us in our own eyes. And what solemn receptions and celebrations with speeches and recitations of poetry he arranged for us whenever he got a medal or a promotion! I still can't forget the striking impression he made at one of those ceremonies due to his extraordinary resourcefulness and tact.

A student in the senior class had come out to the middle of the auditorium to deliver a speech he had prepared. But he had only managed to say, "Your Excellency, Mr. Director," when he lost his nerve and, horribly embarrassed, stood rooted to the spot, lowered his head, and couldn't go on. It was an agonizing moment for everyone there . . . And the director? He got up from the presiding officer's chair, went up to the embarrassed student, put his hand on his shoulder, and said loudly and solemnly:

"My friend! Your silence is more eloquent than the most splendid words. The embarrassment that shows on your young, modest, and pious face clearly testifies to the profound feelings that grip your pure, sinless heart, and this does you honor. Your lowered glance tells me more clearly than words what you meant to tell me in the name of your comrades, with regard to the royal favor of which I have happily been deemed worthy. And therefore be not downcast, my friend: you have already made your speech, and I have heard it. Take from me, as a token of my gratitude, this kiss,—and may it flow out to the hearts of your comrades here present, whom I love as children entrusted to my care and whom you love as your brothers! . . ."

And throwing a kiss to all of us, he went back to his seat to the thunderous applause of the entire adult audience. And as for us students, we were so touched by this episode that our eyes filled with tears of emotion.

I could also write at length about our summer excursions to the country, for "scientific purposes," i.e., for plotting maps and our joyful "May Days" with music, circus performances, and acrobats, to which the local gentry came in their carriages and the other classes came on foot, along with their offspring and domestics. The whole town talked about these "May Days" for a week! Nothing like this happened under the directors that followed him. That is why we respected him, were proud of him, and had it not been for our superstitious fear of him, we would have loved him, despite the fact that the rations assigned us by the government were given to us only in part and that we often felt really deprived, almost starving.

One Sunday, at ten o'clock in the morning, a pre-arranged signal from the doorman's room let us know that the minister had arrived within the walls of the school.

Our hearts pounded, our faces turned pale, many of us had trouble breathing. The decisive moment had come.

The director, in uniform and wearing his regalia, surrounded by the entire school administration, consisting of the inspector, the senior supervisor and the room supervisors, and the school doctor and clerk, met the minister at the school gate.

We simply did not recognize our director. As recently as yesterday he had been a bent down, crumpled, pathetic old man who could hardly move his feet. Today he was a fresh, cheerful, and supremely presentable middle-aged man with a proud carriage, without a single wrinkle on a face radiant with health, and without a single gray hair on his head. We even thought that on this day he seemed to be taller than his usual height and less bony. Since early morning his voice had resounded in the yard and the corridors like a war trumpet. It made everyone tremble—the supervisors, the guards, and all those to whom he issued his short, peremptory commands. We had never known him to have such a loud, sonorous, and healthy voice. Such rapid, surprising metamorphoses occurred with him frequently, and on demand: not for nothing had he been a pupil of the Jesuits. And we, who were obsessed with the heroes of Eugène Sue's *The Wandering Jew*, frequently called him Rodin and sometimes thought seriously, "God knows, maybe he really is a general of the fearsome Jesuits." We were all the more inclined to think so because we sometimes met him in such places and under such circumstances and in such clothing that we no longer doubted that he must be pursuing some secret aims, especially in view of the fact that at such encounters he pretended that he didn't know us at all. When we took off our caps in front of him, he looked straight at us with what seemed to be an unfeigned expression of perplexity and shrugged his shoulders, as if to say "I swear to God I don't know you and can't understand why you are showing me such respect." That is why we felt toward him a sort of unreasoning, superstitious fear.

The minister proceeded to the senior classroom. Filled with an ardent desire to keep *au courant* of what would happen there, we at once selected from our ranks a scout, who was to look through the keyhole and tell us what was going on in the senior classroom, so that we would know how to behave when our tum came.

The information that we received—by means of a very accurately organized postal service—ran sequentially as follows:

—V. (one of the pupils in the senior class) pronounced a prayer in Hebrew before the beginning of class, at the command of the minister.

"That means he is pious," we concluded, and immediately practiced a prayer, along with *The Russian Imperial House* which also might be required.

—M. (the best student in the whole school) greeted the minister with a speech in Latin.

This news inspired us to practice mentally the conjugation of the verb *amare*.

—They are reading the class exercises on Russian literature, and the minister is listening attentively, said the third report.

Some eight minutes passed without any further information. Our curiosity grew with every second. Something important must have happened. Burning with impatience to find out what had occurred, we couldn't wait for the return of our courier and were about to send a second one. But at that moment the first one rushed in.

"Here is what minister said, word for word," he stammered in a husky, unsteady voice.

We pricked up our ears and opened our mouths, so as not to miss a single word.

"Gentlemen, I am astonished," said the minister. "Why this is an institution of higher learning, a university! Your seminarians are university students, and one could not demand anything more advanced from real university students. All the topics are philosophical and have been treated with exemplary knowledge of the subject; it is evident how well read they are. And I had thought that a rabbinical seminary would be . . . an elementary school in which besides Jewish subjects only Russian grammar would be studied. I repeat, gentlemen: I am astonished. I did not at all expect what I am seeing."

Finally our scout returned too, since the minister had proceeded to another class. "Well, how did it go?" we asked him, surrounding him on all sides.

"I think it went all right, he answered, although his response was somehow lacking in confidence. "It came off satisfactorily."

"The minister was satisfied?"

"I think he was satisfied. They all answered very well. The minister only corrected the stresses on words a few times."

"Did he thank anybody?"

"No. He said 'Good' and 'Very good,' but as for thanking, he didn't thank anybody. But maybe he did and I just didn't hear it."

"How about the director?"

"The director is pensive and downcast. The minister very seldom addressed him; he kept talking to N***a I***ch (the Russian literature teacher)."

"A bad sign," we thought.

The minister entered our classroom. We saw before us a still hale, rather portly old man, of above medium height, slightly stooped, and broad-shouldered, with a short neck which supported a small and lean head, which seemed out of keeping with the substantial roundness of his whole torso. His hair, dark brown considerably streaked with gray, was cut short; his face was smooth, white, aristocratic, and good-natured, with a slight flush, and might have been considered open if it hadn't been for his small eyes, which kept looking down. His movements were slow and languid; his voice was throaty, but quiet, with nothing peremptory or imposing about it. In general, he made on us the impression not of a high official, but of a private visitor, a magnate with just a touch of monastic humility, the more so that he was dressed very modestly: a black suit of an old-fashioned cut, with a star; a carelessly tied necktie around his neck; a watch, perhaps of silver, on a faded silk fob; black gloves, simple ones, the kind you can get for thirty kopeks. The effect of all this was that we stopped feeling shy in front of him. We felt at ease and even cheerful at heart. Why our administration was so timid and walking on tiptoe we didn't understand.

"We wish you good health, Your Grace!" we chanted in one voice, in military fashion.

The minister smiled good-naturedly and made a slight bow, but without raising his eyes to us, and kept looking at the ground.

N***ta I***ch came running up, more animated than anyone and in the best of form, probably because the minister had approved of his teaching. As for the director, he stood at a distance, silently watching, as if he were only an observer. A proud, almost contemptuous expression never left his face, which was raised high over the sewn collar of his sixth-class uniform. His right wrist, covered by a white suede glove, seemed frozen into a triangle under his left armpit. He stood like a cast statue, without moving or blinking, and he looked very good in this pose—much more imposing, at least, than the minister, whose simplicity and ordinariness surprised us, though it can't be said that it pleased us very much: we preferred solemnity, official dignity, and the kind of theatrical effects that speak to the imagination. The director had taught us that, and it was right of him to do so, for it accustomed us to orderliness and purified our taste. It did no harm to hold the graduates of a disorderly heder to a strict standard of official orderliness and external decorum, which was supposed to instill in us respect for what had been severely neglected in our previous schooling. Carefree slovenliness could be expunged only by refined orderliness. Whether the director acted consciously, with purpose conceived beforehand on the basis of pedagogical principles, I don't know; but that is the way he acted. Those who came after him and acted differently did great harm to the school in many respects.

"What are you studying with them here?" the minister asked N***ta I***ch.

"Rhetoric and poetics. Besides that, I am developing their style. They write on assigned topics and make translations. Would Your Grace care to hear them recite?"

"All right," the minister replied.

The teacher rushed up to me and whispered in my ear: "From the Triumphal Hymn of the Russians," i.e., a poem whose author was standing there in front of us. My heart pounded from this extraordinary circumstance, but I nevertheless began loudly and distinctly:

> Your knees, O Russians, bend them down
> In pious chorus all together!
> Fix thoughts and minds on Heaven's crown;
> Send thund'ring praise to our Creator!

At the end of the "thund'ring praise" line the minister stopped me, waved his hand, and even scowled. It may have been my intonation that he did not like, or perhaps he considered it tactless to have his own poem recited in front of him—which the teacher probably intended as an act of flattery, but which turned out to be way over the top. At any rate the minister proposed that I recite a different poem.

I began to declaim "A Bard in the Camp of Russian Warriors" with special feeling, since this was one of my favorite poems.[11]

"Good," said the minister, placing his hand on my shoulder when I had recited a few stanzas. "What period is the subject of that poem?"

"The Fatherland War of '12."

"Of which century?"

"The nineteenth," the examinee replied.

"In which other century was the year twelve celebrated?"

"In the seventeenth, after the Time of Troubles."

"Very good," came the minister's praise.

Thus the examination passed over into Russian history. The minister spaced out his questions, jumping from century to century, and we answered briefly and clearly, not making a single slip in chronology.

"All right, children," the minister said. "I am well satisfied with you. I shall tell the sovereign about your successes. Honor to you and glory," he went on, addressing the history teacher, and made him a deep bow.

"I try to do my best, Your Grace," replied the teacher, blushing with joy, and bowed to the waist to the minister.

"And what are they?" asked the minister, pointing to some notebooks lying on the desk.

"Class exercises," answered the literature teacher.

"And drawings," added the teacher of drawing and sketching, a Pole who couldn't speak a word of Russian and had suddenly rushed up from somewhere.

"Do they also draw?"

"Of course they do," he said in Polish, but with some Russian thrown in. "They draw from models. They are lazybones, but they have ability."

Everyone present smiled. The director cast a vicious, annihilating glance at the drawing teacher, a frightful eccentric and fanatic of his art. The teacher fell to licking his lips and smoothing his disheveled hair, muttering to himself. He then retired to the place from which he had jumped out like an unchained animal.

The minister spent a minute or so leafing through the notebooks and then passed them to a ministry official who was accompanying him. The latter put them in his enormous briefcase.

Thus ended the ministerial visit to our class. Nothing special happened in the other classes, and at half past eleven the minister departed from the school. Dinner at half past two was served to us again according to the "discretion" principle and not from the "Prescribed Menu."

VII

Strange. Despite the fact that everything seemed to have "gone well," and the minister had not found a single flaw, once he had left, the administration and the teachers began to walk around as if they had been dunked in water, as if they had somehow messed up. Because of the close intellectual and moral bond that then existed between the teachers and the taught, the teachers' gloom was at once communicated to us—and we too became sad and anxious—for the time being without any visible cause or reason. We somehow did not feel right at heart, although we didn't know whether we should be afraid and what we should be afraid of. Burning with impatience to know what it was all about and what lay ahead for us, we turned to the more popular instructors with direct and indirect questions about the subject that interested us, but did not receive any sort of definite answer. The teachers either stubbornly kept silent or spoke so evasively that we couldn't understand anything. Only one of the supervisors somewhat gratified our curiosity.

"There are going to be a lot of changes here," he once said.

"What sort of changes?"

"All kinds."

"Namely?"

"Wait a bit and you'll see. All in good time. Give it some time."

We allowed plenty of time, but finally the time ran out.

Six or seven weeks after the departure of the minister the school received from St. Petersburg some very important papers. We students of course did not read these papers in the original, but their contents did not remain a secret from us. Their meaning was that "giving full credit to the ability and zeal of the teachers and the diligence, perseverance, and talents of the pupils, the minister finds that the intellectual development that the latter are receiving within the walls of the school does not correspond to the special vocations (as rabbis and teachers) to which they will have to devote themselves within Jewish communities after they leave the school. Therefore it is not at all in accordance with the aims and views of the higher authorities. In particular, the minister cannot condone that dangerous spirit of Western *rationalism* which is to be found in the students' written exercises. In view of their future spiritual calling, students should be educated in that spirit of strict religiosity and patriotic feeling which alone adorns both individual and citizen. Therefore, in order to uproot this dangerous rationalism, which cannot be tolerated in a well-ordered state, swift and decisive measures must be taken."

What sort of a beast this was, the rationalism that the minister had detected in our exercise-books, we didn't know for sure. But that it must be very dangerous we understood from the changes that swiftly followed, one after the other.

The director, in view of his advanced years, was forced to retire. The teacher of Russian literature, who had been given a medal, was transferred to a gymnasium—*the gymnasium* students were evidently insulated against rationalism. The mathematics teacher was at last *allowed* to transfer to service in the Institute of Nobility, which he had long been petitioning for, but always without success. The teacher of history and geography, who had once taught law in the gymnasium, was now assigned to teach Greek there; therefore he would not have time to give lessons in our school. The Latin teacher was effectively dismissed in that his very subject was eliminated. Latin was eliminated in order to block the graduates of a rabbinical seminary from attending institutions of higher education, which they might, in the course of their development, conceive a desire to enter. O sancta simplicitas! As if a young lad aiming for higher education could be held back by the lack of one or two subjects! And in fact it did happen that rabbinical seminarians by the dozen later entered institutions of higher education, taking supplementary examinations in subjects not taught in the rabbinical seminaries ... In short, the body of teachers of general subjects was disbanded, and for the time being, pending the appointment of new ones, instruction was entrusted to certain private teachers from the town, almost taken off the street ... The *mules* and the laggards were triumphant.

Such was the fate of the teachers. As for us students, in order to uproot rationalism from among us and to implant religious and patriotic feelings, the following orders came down from on high:

Strengthen instruction in Jewish subjects; stop lending books for reading from the school library; when presenting subjects, hold strictly to established programs and textbooks; require the inspector to attend our early morning prayers and read aloud to us in class brochures sent from the ministry in Hebrew and German entitled "On Respect for the Tsar" and "On Those of Different Faiths." In addition, on Saturdays and holidays pupils in receipt of state support must go to pray in the Great Synagogue; there too, on national holidays, they must stay behind after their prayers to hear the sermon of the city preacher, who is to receive compensation of twenty roubles for each sermon. And so on, in the same vein.

A new regime was established, a new spirit was felt—a putrid and deadening one. Fanatics (among the Jewish teachers there were such) raised their heads and began to instill fear not only among the students, but also among their progressive colleagues. The latter lowered their heads, began to act sanctimonious, play the hypocrite, and sing in unison with triumphant ignorance and obscurantism. Punctilious Jewish ceremonialism became predominant, and we grew sick to death of it, the more so as we had gotten completely out of the habit of it. Jewish teachers stood on guard in the dining room during our repasts to make sure that we carried out the obligatory washing of hands, recitation of dinner-table prayers, and so forth. Sudden inspections were carried out of our *tallit katan* vests to determine whether we were wearing the ritual tassels or fringes (tzitzit) required by the rules. If these were missing, we would be fined, one conduct point would be deducted, and any reward already earned would be cancelled. In a word, it was clerical terror, and what is saddest of all, this terror, whether sincerely or hypocritically, was zealously supported even by those of our Jewish teachers who had hitherto been known as enlightened progressives, advanced activists, and even writers.

A single happy exception was the unforgettable A. B. Lebenson,[12] a poet and thinker and, most of all, a man of unshakable firmness and profound convictions, consistent in both thought and action, disdainful of cowardly compromises with his own solid conscience. He gave no recognition to the new regime, did not bow to triumphant obscurantism, gave no support to the fanatics and bigots, but forced them out into the open. Without entering into heated arguments or fulsome polemics, since by nature he was quiet, modest, even-tempered, and taciturn, self-contained like a true philosopher, on occasion he would fire at them a single short, but clear riposte, and this brief sally was enough to shut their mouths and make them retreat. Even the most ardent fanatics gave way before Lebenson. They were afraid of him as if he embodied their *memento mori*, since for him it would be only a minute's work fully to expose all their intellectual and moral worthlessness as well as their impenetrable ignorance. They were all the more ready to lay down their arms in front of him because he was a man with an irreproachable past and a spotless present, able to look them straight in the eye, while they, for their part, could not do that, since their past had on it various spots and fissures . . . Lebenson was our only consolation, our only moral support in the painful time that had begun for us, and we rallied around him like sailors around the mast of a ship sinking to the bottom. We had always loved and respected him, but now we came to adore him. His moral influence on us became enormous, and this influence kept us from despair, demoralization, and from any wavering in our convictions. We drew apart from the other Jewish teachers; our previous patriarchal relations with them ceased, and their authority in our eyes declined decisively. The true fanatics among them we came to despise, and the hypocrites we hated. Later, when the reign of official obscurantism began little by little to weaken and subside, they began to play up to us, to flatter us, hoping once again to win our confidence, but they did not succeed. They had lost our confidence forever; the diminished credit of those chameleons could no longer be restored by any means.

One amusing episode from the time of that obscurantist regime has remained in my memory. It is lodged there all the more firmly because I myself played a certain role in it, or more accurately, I was the cause of it.

As I mentioned earlier, according to the prescriptions of the ministry students with state support in a rabbinical seminary on Saturdays and holidays had to go pray in the Great Synagogue and on national holidays to listen to the sermons of the city preacher. So we went and listened, that is, listened to rubbish and nonsense which we were bound to dislike, because we were used to coherent exposition of ideas. We especially disliked the sermons of the city preacher, who was an excellent Talmudist, but a poor speaker and evidently gave his improvisations unwillingly and carelessly. But that was nothing. You could stand and avoid listening to the preacher's nasal twang, think about something else, or examine the frescoes in the cupola over the synagogue platform, remarkable in their way. I don't think a single architect or sculptor could fully understand those frescoes; they were extraordinarily intricate, complicated, almost inexplicable. On the branches of trees of uncertain species were perched some animals— they could have been lions, or perhaps leopards, but they looked very much like clipped poodles; over their heads some bullocks with stag horns and wings on their backs were galloping past. In the bushes there crawled snakes with bushy tails, feathers for swimming, and heads with bird beaks. In short, what was represented here in figures was a natural scene that no scientist ever dreamed of, even one suffering from delirium tremens or some other disease of the brain. Consequently there was something to look at, and you didn't have to listen. And we really didn't listen—and that was a good thing.

The only trouble was that the governor general, I. G. Bibikov,[13] who was at the same time trustee of the school district, for some reason suddenly wanted to know what the preacher was preaching to us. So orders were issued here and there, as a result of which the preacher received instructions to reproduce his sermons on paper after he had given them, so that they could later be translated into Russian. But since the preacher, in view of his advanced age could no longer manage a pen very well, a clerk attached to him did the writing. Since that clerk was not a very literate person, he spilled onto the paper whatever God put in his head. That *paper* was sent to the school and given to the senior class for translation. But there was nothing really to translate, since the sermon consisted of an utterly formless collection of biblical verses and Talmudic pronouncements without any logical or literary connection. So the senior class would then take it upon itself to compose a sermon according to all the rules of rhetoric, with a *beginning*, *middle*, and *end*, and with appropriate quotations from the Bible, the Talmud, the midrash, etc.

"The governor general read the sermon in its entirety and liked it very much," the director told us when he returned from making his report. "He ordered me to thank the preacher and to tell him to continue to teach you in such words, which each time I should present to him in translation."

The preacher, flattered and encouraged by the governor general's gratitude, did not have to be asked again, the more so that for each sermon he expected a reward of twenty rubles, a rather sizable sum at that time, especially in view of the wretched salary he got from the congregation. Therefore he began to flood the school with *papers* which had to be transformed into correct sermons, such as he had never delivered. Since this work turned out to be more than the senior class could perform by itself, some of it was passed on to other classes, including ours of course.

At first this work engaged us in the sense that we used it for exercising and trying out our talents in religious rhetoric, which would be useful to us later, in our future capacity as rabbis. But little by little the senior class began to shirk the task under various high-sounding pretexts, and we ended up saddled with it all. The lion's share of the job the director kindly allocated to me, since I had already acquired mastery of the pen and was therefore *obliged* to carry on my shoulders the honor of the school in the eyes of the governor general, who had become intensely interested in Jewish sermons, almost acquiring a passion for them. No matter how many the director brought him, he read them all.

I became downcast. The job was crushing me and taking up almost all my time. I had barely coped with one *paper* when the director would send me another, received "for translation" from the city preacher. But what the devil was there to translate when the sermon lacked a single coherent sentence or a single logical thought? I had to invent and compose it all. To become a composer of imaginary sermons was not at all what I had planned. What was I to do, how could I rid myself of this stupid job? I thought and thought and finally got the answer.

Once when I had received a *paper* from the director "for translation," I simply translated it word for word, neither adding nor subtracting anything.

I remember that paper contained references to marinated herring, a greased wheel, a sack with holes in it, Uriah the Hittite, worn-out shoes, Balaam's ass, and other such nonsense. All this was interlarded in the most amazing way with quotations which had nothing to do with the topic at hand, and I translated all that rubbish, holding my sides with laughter as I did so. When the translation was ready, I delivered it to the director, who without reading it headed off to see governor general, taking it and some other sermons with him . . .

Not half an hour had passed before the director rushed into the school, red-faced, embarrassed, and angry. I was at once summoned to the teachers' lounge. When I entered, my manuscript was being passed from hand to hand, and all the teachers were convulsed with laughter. The director, however, was not laughing, but was furious.

"Is this your work?" he asked, grabbing my manuscript from the hands of one of the teachers and throwing it on the table.

"It is."

"Are you in your right mind?"

"As usual."

"Why on earth did you cook up all this rubbish?"

"I wasn't the one who cooked it up—its author did. I only translated what was in the original, and for the accuracy of the translation I'll answer with my head."

"Why wasn't there nonsense like this in previous translations?"

"Because they were not translations. We didn't translate, we created. We composed sermons that the preacher never delivered and will never deliver."

"So that's the way it is!" exclaimed the director, snapping his fingers. Now I understand. And was it like that from the beginning?"

"From the very beginning."

"Why didn't anyone warn me? You put me in a very awkward position with the governor general. I didn't know what to say to him."

"For that I am really guilty, and I ask your forgiveness."

"Gentlemen," the director turned to the teachers. "What am I to say to the governor general? He is expecting an explanation." He roared with laughter, snorted and spat and then sent me away to investigate. Now I am under strict orders to come right back to him and explain what happened with this sermon.

"Just explain simply what happened, and that will be the end of it," was the advice of the teachers. "He will laugh, and that will be all."

The director did exactly that. The consequence of this "adventure" was that despite the prescriptions of the minister, the governor general on his own authority liberated us from the requirement of listening to the sermons of the city preacher, and the latter ceased to weary us with those papers of his, which we had wasted so much time reworking—and so unproductively at that . . .

VIII

It would, of course, be strange to think or claim that someone somewhere had, *from higher considerations*, deliberately chosen and assigned to us teachers that were beneath all criticism; but that is what it looked like.

The man appointed as teacher of Russian language and literature was a Pole, a graduate in law, who read Russian with a foreign accent, made grammatical mistakes when writing, and hadn't the slightest notion of literature, his supposed subject. Right away, from the very first lesson, he placed his subject at the *level* at which certain people somewhere wanted to see it . . . Without beating around the bush, he made a brief and clear statement to the effect that he intended to stick strictly to the textbooks and was not going to study with us any *extracurricular* readings. This mode of instruction suited him particularly because, as we noticed, he was bored by teaching, did not like his subject, liked to play the dandy, and circulated in higher Polish society, where his specialty was dancing. After dancing all night at balls, he would come to class the next day exhausted, pale, and sleepy. He would ask questions right out of the book and make assignments the same way, without giving any explanations or asking for any. With the former teacher we had been used to preparing written exercises for each class, but we quickly got out of that habit, since the dancer, if he collected our notebooks at all, kept them for months on end, and then either returned them without any corrections or did not return them at all; frequently he simply lost them. From this we understood that whereas these exercises had been a matter of primary concern for our former teacher, this teacher was only bored by them, and so we decided not to bore him anymore. He was satisfied, and we were satisfied, the more so that he was a man of the greatest refinement, who gave us good marks, and in general treated us with exquisite politeness, which could not be said of the former teacher, who was a graduate of a seminary, that is, an ex-divinity student and son of an Orthodox priest.

One day our dancer pleasantly surprised us with a *literary* discussion, of the following kind:

"Yesterday I got sad news from Moscow," he announced in an unctuous tone, stroking his magnificent mane of hair, and blushing because he was not used to talking to us in such a personal way. "Gogol has died.[14] There was a writer by that name."

"We know him," we replied, hinting that we didn't need at all to be told who Gogol was.

"That is, personally?" the teacher asked.

"No, from his works."

"But I knew him personally. I use to meet him in society, at the home of Count Tolstoy.[15] What works of his have you read?"

"All of them that have been published."

"There is still another work that has not yet appeared in print, the 'Author's Confession.'[16] It is circulating in manuscript. A remarkable work."

We of course took him at his word and only asked him to describe what Gogol looked like and what his habits were. He satisfied our curiosity, and for that we were very grateful.[17]

"And you, so-and-so, you write poetry," he said to me with a gracious smile. "Write an elegy 'On the Death of Gogol.'"

For the next lesson I brought to class a poem which began:

> *Of yet one more far-sighted prophet*
> *Has mother Rus' now been deprived*

The teacher loudly and solemnly read the poem aloud to the whole class in a singsong voice, stood up and bowed to me as a sign of praise and gratitude. He then put the poem in his side pocket, from where sure enough it vanished without trace.

Our new teacher of history and geography was no better an acquisition. He was a graduate of the main pedagogical institute, a Swede or Finn by origin, a good-natured, merry, but terribly stupid young man. And as for telling lies— lying was his forte; he loved it and was a master at it! We didn't doubt that if he were not actually Nozdryov[18] in person, he was at least his brother or nephew. Straight off he told us openly that he was a bit weak in universal history, but as far as Russian history was concerned he was a pupil of Ustryalov[19] and so a real expert, and that in two years' time, when he finished his dissertation, he would receive a professorship. So at first he undertook to initiate us into "the art of writing history from sources." For this purpose he brought to class with him publications by the Archeographic Commission,[20] taught us to read the

chronicles, wrote commentaries on them, and subjected them to historical criticism—in short, he did a load of different bits and pieces with us, imagining
that he was a professor working with advanced students. As for universal history, he harshly criticized and ridiculed Smaragdov,[21] reducing him to dust and
ashes, and advised us to prepare our lessons from notes we could make ourselves
from German textbooks, since we read German quite easily. So we did exactly
that, pleased and flattered that the teacher had such confidence in our intellectual maturity and considered it beneath our dignity to hold us to rote memo-
rization.

But little by little he began to cool off, both toward his work with us on Russian history and also toward our independent *labors* on universal history. He began coming to class without any sources. He would walk back and forth, yawning occasionally, and spluttering in his discontent. Sometimes he would ask us
about the lesson, sometimes not. As for assignments, he would limit himself to
saying, a minute before the bell rang:

"For next time do what comes next."

By making some inquiries we learned that he had begun drinking and play-
ing cards for nights on end. We gave up on him and came to the conclusion that
in effect we had no history teacher. It went so far that when he asked us to recite
someone would stand up, pick up the first book that came to hand,—it might
have been a novel or an anthology, and would read aloud until he got tired, and
would then turn the book over to another student. This passed for a history lesson: the teacher was completely distracted and inattentive in class.

Once it even happened that some student asked what was *Tilly* (he was
one of the army commanders during the Thirty Years' War).[22] The teacher just
barked out:

"Go look on the map; it must be somewhere in Germany."

In his more lucid moments he told us anecdotes, one more improbable and
absurd than the next.

As for the new mathematics teacher, we didn't know what to think about
him. He was some sort of automaton, a mannequin, whose phlegmatic nature,
lack of feeling, and indifference were beyond belief. He was said to know his subject very well, but he taught it dully, lifelessly, mechanically, without the least interest in whether the students learned or didn't. After teaching for three months
he still didn't know a single pupil either by sight or by name, nor what class he
was in. This gave the lower classes the opportunity to play some incredible tricks
on him. We, i.e., the students in our class, didn't play any tricks, but during his
classes we did our own thing—one read books, another wrote letters home, still

another would take off his jacket and sew on a missing button, and yet another would stretch himself out on the bench, sleeping the sleep of the just, complete with snores. The teacher seemed to observe all this, yet he didn't see it at all; at least he never expressed any displeasure, as if it were all quite expected and natural. He stood at the blackboard, drawing geometric figures and writing algebraic formulas, without ever asking whether we understood what he was doing or not. If he called on us from his class list, the person called on would answer "Absent" and go back to what he had been doing.

"Then who is sitting here in class?" the teacher would ask.

"We don't know," we would answer without blinking.

This reply passed for a normal response. As for marks, he assigned them either completely at random or by copying the marks the student received in other courses: good students got good marks; bad students, bad ones. If a student were dissatisfied with his mark, he would protest:

"Last week you questioned me, and I gave excellent answers," the protester would lie without blushing.

"Really?" the teacher would ask submissively and timidly.

"The whole class can testify to it," the pupil would continue boldly, knowing very well that the whole class could testify that the entire previous week he had not been to the mathematics class even once.

"I'm sorry," the teacher would say and correct the mark.

Such an original cohort of teachers of the most important subjects of instruction—a cohort which suited all the *mules* and laggards perfectly—was the topic of endless conversations, speculations, and lamentations by the more serious and diligent students, who could not become reconciled to the fact that their time was being wasted unproductively, and that they were not making any progress in their educational development. The distress of these students was especially acute and well-founded because they knew very well that the rabbinical seminary would be the last stage in their education, that this was the end of the road for them. Sometimes it seemed to them that this cohort of teachers had been put together by accident, in which case they had only fate to blame; but more often they came to the conclusion that such teachers had not been gathered by chance, but selected on purpose, so that instruction in the school would be conducted limply and haphazardly. If that were true, no extenuating circumstances could limit their fury.

It was the feelings of the best students in the school on this score that made me choose as the subject for my play the bad students at a certain institution of higher education. Hence my play was entitled *The Would-Be Teacher.*

IX

The parts had been copied out and assigned, and the actors set about their business with zeal. The *committee* members, for their part, took to their own duties with even more zeal—the mise en scène, costumes, stage properties, and so forth. One of the classrooms—one more distant from the eyes of the watchful authorities—was turned into a real workshop, in which anyone who had the slightest capacity for any sort of trade found employment. The cost of supplies was covered by voluntary contributions, and no one was stingy. The devotion to the common cause was extraordinary. And, to avoid any problems from the watchmen responsible for the classrooms, which included the very room we had chosen as our theater space, the committee entered into negotiations with them in advance. These negotiations arrived at a very successful conclusion: the watchmen promised that on the day of the performance they would give us all the keys; they only begged us, for the love of God, not to start a fire.

Everyone felt happy, triumphant, and exultant in advance: the *actors*, sure that they would excel, and the *public*, who were expecting an entertaining show. I was the only one who walked around totally downcast, rumpling my hair, and wringing my hands. This was because I was terribly scared of appearing before the public with this *creation* of mine. No matter how often those who had read the play assured me that it was good and interesting, in my own mind I was somehow convinced that people wouldn't like it. It would be ridiculed, hissed, and booed. So at that time my most ardent wish was that some unexpected problem would arise so that our whole undertaking would be scuttled and I wouldn't have to submit to the judgement of a public whose verdict I feared more than death itself. For some reason I thought that my whole fate rested on this debut, and I cursed myself in thought for having jumped at my comrades' bait and cooked up such a stew, a stew I hated so much that I would have paid dearly for it not to have existed at all. My insecurity and timidity as the fateful moment approached got so bad that I seriously considered whether it wouldn't be right to ask my comrades tearfully to take pity on me and call the project off. Alternatively, I could invoke my rights as the author, recall the play and forbid its performance. In any case, I had made a firm decision not to be present at the performance. If the play was destined to be a flop, let it happen out of my sight, or else I couldn't bear it, especially since among the public I had plenty of ill-wishers, people who envied me, enemies both secret and open, whom I had never spared myself and who would not spare me now . . .

Then one *actor* after another came up to me and asked me to listen to the way he read his part, was the emphasis in the right place, and so forth. And as if to spite and tempt me, every one of them read his part with feeling, with love, with self-awareness, and with full conviction that his part was one of the best in the play and that he would create a sensation with it! What was I to think about my play? Wasn't it cowardice on my part to think it would be a flop? But on the other hand, why did my heart tell me, why did it have this foreboding that it would surely be a failure? In short, I experienced all the forebodings, doubts, fears, and hopes that a real dramatist goes through at the first performance of a real play on a real stage.

At last the great day of the performance arrived. We had deliberately picked a day when an old watchman was on duty whose vigilance we could more easily cope with.

Beginning early in the morning the committee, reinforced with a dozen robust apprentices, began to transform one of the classrooms into a theater. Several sheets were taken off our bunks and transformed into a curtain in the twinkling of an eye. The other preparations went just as fast, with the result that by noon everything was ready, and the students began to await the evening with an impatience which was easy to understand. And to gain more time, we set the school clocks ahead by two hours, so that when it was eight o'clock in the evening in the town, in the school it was already ten. The old watchman hurried us off to bed, and this time we didn't wait to be asked twice.

"That's the way! That's what I like!" he said, rubbing his hands, when he saw that we were heading for the dormitory without argument or dispute.

We all threw ourselves onto our bunks without getting undressed, wrapped ourselves in our blankets, put out the candles, and pretended to be asleep. When one of the apprentices assigned for reconnaissance at the guardroom door snapped his fingers to let us know that the old watchman had already gone to sleep, we all together jumped off our bunks and quietly, on tiptoe, left the dormitories, and made our way to the theater. I alone stood in the darkness by my bunk, undecided and unsure whether to go or not. But curiosity won out over my other calculations, and I went.

When I entered, everything was in order. The room was brightly lit by several dozen candle stubs, which for a week the students had been carefully collecting for the occasion. The curtain with the muse Cleo in the middle solemnly, mysteriously, and full of promise concealed what soon would appear before us as a stage setting. The watchman Justin, shaven, combed, and wearing a jacket with metal buttons and a blue collar, was standing at one edge of the curtain as if he had been sewn to it, ready at a signal to raise it using a rope, one end of which he was holding tightly in both hands. He was very serious, recognizing the seriousness of his mission. Two steps from the curtain, along its whole length stretched a row of chairs—for the students of the senior class, our "honored guests," who had taken no part at all in our whole undertaking, but who were to *honor* the performance with their presence. These "learned and serious scholars," whom we respected deeply, were sitting in a dignified manner and from time to time whispering among themselves. O, if only *they* would like it, I thought, I need no greater happiness. Their presence reassured me considerably, since their attitude toward me was benevolent, and they wouldn't permit any scandal . . . The rest of the *public* was seated on benches, placed in amphitheater style behind the chairs.

I made my way to the very last bench, crammed myself into a corner and sat down with my heart pounding. I felt a pounding in my temples too. There was a solemn silence. You could hear the sputtering of the candle-ends in their candlesticks, the heavy breathing of Justin, who was not used to having his jacket all buttoned up, and the swift steps of the *actors* behind the *scenery flats*, i.e., in the room adjacent to the stage. The minutes felt to me like hours, days, months.

At last, at a signal given behind the stage, Justin spat into both palms and gave the rope a vigorous jerk. The rope remained in his hands, while he himself ended up lying prostrate on the floor, in the process knocking over a chair, which fortunately was empty. But nevertheless the curtain did rise.

There was a friendly outburst of laughter, after which the solemn silence resumed, accompanied by acute attentiveness. I considered the episode with the rope a bad omen for me and braced myself with stoicism to endure further storms and misfortunes . . . But when the *public* cast their eyes over the half-lit stage and saw Rosenroth rising from his bunk, in his student uniform, beautifully made up, with a notebook in one hand, and a lit cigarette in the other, the hall resounded with bursts of deafening applause, and I felt a little better at heart.

However much Rosenroth had counted on applause, such an overwhelming reception at his first appearance before the public, when he had not yet managed to say a single word, exceeded all his expectations, and he was taken aback and even frightened, which was at once reflected on his thin face, which turned now red, now pale from the emotions that agitated him. But he swiftly got control of his feelings, and throwing his notebook on the desk and striding around the stage, he began his soliloquy, "O these damned professors!" The public were all ears, held their breath, and opened their mouths, swallowing every phrase. At the transparent allusions to circumstances familiar to all they remarked aloud,

"We understand," and at the more subtle ones, "We'll ask the author later." At every joke they would roar with hearty guffaws, and when the *actor*, carried away, began to talk too fast, they would stop him, saying: "Slow down, Rosenroth, nobody's chasing you." Sometimes Rosenroth obeyed the public's commands, but sometimes he stuck out his tongue or made a ludicrous face and kept going. When the second actor sang the couplet, "When things for you are going badly," the public became so ecstatic that the performance was halted and almost stopped altogether, threatening to turn into a battle between the audience and the actors.

The trouble was that first the public would applaud loudly and cry "Bravo!" The actor would bow and shuffle his feet. Then the public would begin to shout "*Bis!*" The actor would sing the couplet again. Again applause and cries of "Bravo!"

"Again!" the public demanded.

"Again?" the actor would retort, making a face, "Some other time."

"Not some other time, now."

"I don't want to."

"But we demand it!"

"But let me go on, or I'll never finish!"

"Then don't finish. You don't need to. Just sing us that couplet."

"I've got another couplet, better than that one: 'Our age is truly a golden one.'"

"All right, let's have it."

"I can't sing it yet."

"Never mind, go ahead."

"You're idiots, you don't understand anything."

"And you're a fool."

"Cock-a-doodle-doo!" someone cried like a rooster, dragging out the cry.

This was a signal for the pranksters and rowdies, who jumped up from their seats and wanted to take over. But at this point the senior class intervened. Subduing, admonishing and shaming the out-of-control ruffians, they restored order, and the performance, which had been on the point of breaking off, continued without any further adventures. The public behaved itself decently, even refraining from making any more comments out loud.

Indignant as I had been over the wild scene that had just taken place, which I had watched from my corner with clenched fists and grinding teeth, my overwhelmingly unpleasant impression was somewhat mitigated by the realization that people had liked my play, that my work had not been in vain, and that no one was going to make me an object of ridicule. And indeed, as soon as the performance was over, *everyone*, absolutely everyone there, not excepting the Olympians of the senior class, rushed up to me with the most enraptured procla-mations of their gratitude for the pleasure I had given them. They embraced me, kissed me, congratulated me. Even people with whom I had long ago broken off all comradely relations made peace with me and offered their friendship.

"All right," I said, making peace with my *enemies*. "Friends, I'm never against friendship. But if you start getting nasty and messing with me again, I'll find a way of getting back at you."

"Now, take it easy," my new friends objected. "We're not going to go over old scores. You're just hot-tempered, but you're basically a good fellow. We've always respected you."

My triumph was complete, so complete that I didn't sleep all night because of the feelings that so pleasantly gripped me.

X

But the next day these pleasant feelings were transformed into feelings quite the opposite. We were faced with the prospect of enduring an onslaught from the fearsome authorities, who had found out about yesterday's contraband enter-tainment. They learned about it from the old watchman, Josef. Josef was a tall, grey old man, a veteran of the former Polish—and subsequently the Russian—army,[23] who remembered the battle of Ostrolenko, grand duke Constantine,[24] Field Marshal Pashkevich of Erevan,[25] Diebitsch Zabalkansky,[26] and other gen-erals, whose names he distorted to the point of unintelligibility, not so much because of illiteracy as from his peculiar sense of humor which was tinged with Polish nationalism.

He was a malicious, spiteful, and crafty old codger, who loved to play the ec-centric, the oddball, sometimes the out-and-out fool, although in fact he always had his wits about him. So much so that although he was already past seventy and was afraid of losing his post because of old age, he married a pretty seven-teen-year-old girl . . . just in case.

"You old fool, what are you doing?" his fellow watchmen reproached him.

"I may be a fool, but I'm smarter than all of you put together," he replied, sniff-ing tobacco and slyly winking one eye. "Fool I may be, but I know how to look out for number one. I know what I am doing."

He knew that a young and beautiful wife would save him from many misfortunes linked to helpless old age, and he made no mistake in his calculations. She really did take care of him, so that he lacked for nothing right up to the day of his death.

Even though he was most assiduous in taking bribes from us "for vodka," he nevertheless snitched on us to the administration whenever he got the chance, the more so that he was very much in the good graces and confidence of the senior supervisor, the highest police authority in the institution, who was also a relative and a veteran of the former Polish army. Every morning he came to the senior supervisor with an oral report, and in the guise of innocent, offhand gossip, told stories about students, watchmen, and anyone else he wanted to spite. That was what happened in our case. He had allowed his palms to be well greased with money "for vodka" and had made no effort to prevent us from doing whatever we liked in the classrooms, but the very next day he reported to the senior supervisor the crimes we had committed.

The senior supervisor came rushing to the school more dead than alive. He was a good, kind, accommodating man, not officious at all, but a great coward, deathly afraid of responsibility. Now he was afraid of being held responsible, since in the absence of the director, who was away on temporary leave, the whole school was under his command, subject to the higher authority of the Inspector of the entire school district. Now suddenly along comes a scandal like this, such a case of criminal wrongdoing! A theatrical performance in a religious school!! It was no joke. He thought that exile to Siberia would be the least he could expect. He had always had a tendency to stutter, but now he was in such a state of agitation that he couldn't pronounce a single word. He ran around the courtyard as if he were on fire, now rushing up to the supervisors standing there, now rushing up to the watchmen, waving his arms in despair. He was trying to say something, but all that came out were sounds: "Bo . . ., bo . . ., bo. . ., vo . . ., vo . . ., to . . ., to . . ., to!" But the main thing was that he was so distracted, in such a state, that he didn't know where to begin or what to do. Finally it occurred to him that first of all he should consult the watchman who had been on duty. The poor old man, trembling like an aspen leaf swore by all that was dear to him, calling God and the heavenly host as his witness, that he was not guilty, that the students had gone to bed, and to sleep at the regular time. How they had pulled off such a stunt he didn't know, because he had dozed off for a moment.

"We-e-ll, er-r, nie trzeba było (you shouldn't have) dozed off!"

They began to investigate the affair thoroughly, who were the "instigators," who had been the actors, and what play they had performed, and so they necessarily worked their way to me; and as the author of the performed play and thus clearly the chief guilty party, of course I was called. To understand how awkward the situation was for the supervisor as judge and me as defendant, you must realize that I had been his favorite of favorites. He had championed me not with his words but with his deeds. In the town he was considered the best teacher of Polish language and literature, subjects he had taught for high fees in the model girls' boarding school and in the foremost aristocratic homes. But to me he had taught these subjects gratis and with remarkable zeal, and had granted me free access to his rich Polish library, which he treasured like the apple of his eye.

Twice a week I was *obliged* to go to his home, where I was received in his family as if I were one of them, a member of the family,—an honor not accorded any other student. We ordinarily greeted one another like relatives, i.e., he kissed me on the forehead and I kissed his hand. Just a few days before he had gone quite out of his mind and wept like a child, almost crushing me in his embrace, when I, wanting to give him a surprise offering as my benefactor and knowing what a passionate Polish patriot he was, had recited by heart in front of his family two long passages from Mickiewicz's *Konrad Wallenrod* and Malczewski's *Maria.*[*] But now, despite what our relations had been, he had to reprimand and judge me, and for my part, I felt that I was almost the chief cause of the danger that was threatening my benefactor! You can easily imagine what we both must have felt on that occasion!

He was sitting in the guard room with his head lowered, wringing his hands, and I was standing like a convicted criminal, having confessed my guilt. We were both silent, not daring to look at one another.

At last he began:

"Well, you have gotten me in a lot of trouble. I am going to catch it, and so are you, but especially me."

"I don't care about myself. Come what may, I am ready for anything," I replied firmly, satisfied that he had spoken out at last. "But I think that you needn't be so worried and alarmed. This matter is essentially a triviality, a prank."

"I too know that it was a prank. But have you forgotten? B. is involved! He's not the kind of person who takes anything as a joke. It's the prison carriage for me, and a soldier's overcoat for you—those are going to be the results of your prank!"

---

[*]   Adam Mickiewicz's *Konrad Wallenrod* and Antoni Malczewsk's *Maria* were two patriotic Polish masterpieces of poetry.

"Now then, things won't go that far."

"How do you know?"

"There is the district inspector. He is a kind man, enlightened, loves our school. He'll plead for us or perhaps quash the whole business."

"And if he's scared and doesn't quash it?"

I didn't know what to reply to that.

"Well, I'll soon find out how he views the matter," said the senior supervisor, looking at his watch. "I have to report to him at ten o'clock."

He ordered Josef to bring him his formal uniform, hat, and gloves, and after saying a prayer before the guardroom reproduction of the Ostrobrama Mother of God, set off at ten o'clock to see the district inspector. On his return he announced that the district inspector would come to the school at twelve o'clock, and therefore the supervisor on duty was ordered not to grant any student permission to go into town.

At noon the district inspector arrived and, accompanied by the senior supervisor, went straight into the office, where I was soon summoned. Realizing that they would need material proofs of our *crime*, I put my unhappy play under my arm and set off for the *courtroom*. I didn't feel especially anxious, in the first place because I was convinced that in essence the whole business wasn't worth all the fuss, and in the second place, because I placed great hopes on the kindness and indulgence of the judge. I based my hope on the fact that I was in the good graces of the district inspector, since he had examined me more than once, praised me, and taken an interest in my literary exercises, which he, ever since the above mentioned teacher-dancer was appointed in our school, himself corrected, always encouraging me to experiment more and more. Besides that, he was in general a kind, indulgent, fair, and humane man, although in appearance he seemed strict, proud, and inaccessible. He frightened people especially with his dry, yellow, gloomy, and perpetually unsmiling face, and with his loud, slow, monotonous voice. It was said of him that he was a great jokester and humorist, who could keep a whole company in stitches for hours on end, but he *recited* his humorous conversations like a sleepy psalm-reader chanting over a corpse. His parchment-like face not only did not smile on such occasions, but kept its permanent gloomy and strict expression. Therefore people who did not know him were as scared of him as if he were a strict, implacable superior; but I knew how deceptive this imposing appearance was. I was not scared and went to the *trial* awaiting me with a light heart. All the same, however, I didn't think I would get off without a reprimand accompanied by more or less harsh, sarcastic comments.

But in that I was mistaken. When I entered the office, I took a few steps and stopped to bow from a distance to the district inspector, who was sitting in the presiding officer's chair. He said in his loud, heavy voice:

"Come close, Mr. Criminal, otherwise I can't see from a distance what sort of expression you have on your face after the crime you have committed."

From that I understood that the district inspector was turning the whole affair into a joke, and casting a glance at the senior supervisor, who was standing at a distance and trembling with his whole body, I went up to the desk.

"All right, show us what you've cooked up."

I handed him my manuscript.

"Aha, you have been trying your hand in the field of drama, have you?" he asked, looking at the title and beginning to leaf through the notebook. "That's fine, that's intelligent. You should test your skill in various genres until you find your true calling. Read it."

I began to read, and he offered corrections, made remarks, and gave instructions, both theoretical and practical. We spent about half an hour in this way.

"Well, that's enough," he said, stopping me. "You have quite a way to go before you become a Shakespeare, but you do have talent. Keep working."

Then, putting on his pince-nez and turning to the supervisor, he said: "Tell me this. According to the charter students are forbidden to attend the theater?"

"They are."

"But this student (pointing at me), and this is an exception not to apply to any others, should be allowed to go to the theater whenever he wants, because he needs the theater. He has signs of literary talent, and he *must* get acquainted with the stage. And as for you, young man," he said, turning to me, "when you write another play, don't have it performed in the school, because that is forbidden by the charter, but bring it to me for approval.

"When you have a play written according to all the rules of dramatic art, we'll have it performed on a local stage."

With that he dismissed me.

"What do you think now? Why were you so worried?" I asked the senior supervisor, after the confrontation had ended so successfully.

Instead of answering, he embraced me, kissed me on the forehead, and from that time began lending me from his library the dramatic works of Count Fredro,[27] Korzeniowski,[28] Bogusławski,[29] and others.

* * *

But despite the most flattering comments of my fellow students about my play, in my own mind I was far from confident about it, since I had not yet heard the verdict of the most competent of the young judges, the gymnasium student Za***cki. Therefore, after entering more corrections and making a fair copy, I sent it to him with a letter asking him to be severe, not to feel constrained by our friendly relations, since I was sending it to him for his judgment, not to solicit insincere praise and compliments. He was true to my request. A week later I got my manuscript back, all sprinkled with corrections, revisions, notes, and marks: weak, unnatural, meaningless, people don't express themselves that way in Russian, nonsense, balderdash, prosody not observed, and so on and so forth, so that in the entire manuscript there was not a single passage left untouched. From this I saw that my work, which had won me so much glory among my undemanding and unsophisticated fellow students, was such an utter piece of rubbish that I was ashamed to keep it among my papers. And therefore, when the time came to light the stoves, with a kind of feverish haste I consigned to one of them my poor *Would-Be Teacher*, from the *actors*, so that no trace would remain of a work of which I was now ashamed as if it were a bad deed that had besmirched my honor. In a sort of fury I stirred *The Would-Be Teacher* from side to side with a poker, pushing it deeper into the fire, and covering it with hot coals, so that the scoundrelly thing would burn up as quickly as possible; and I felt relief and a kind of moral satisfaction only when it had mingled with the ashes from the stove . . .

I sat down to write a new play, swearing not to show it to any of my fellow students or to talk about it, but to keep it in deep secrecy so that no one could even be curious about it or pester me and again lead me astray by inopportune and undeserved praise, which only harms and hinders proper development. But I was obliged to reveal this deepest of secrets, this most private of all matters . . . to the governor general, I. G. Bibikov.

It happened like this. One Saturday, after dinner, when half the students had been allowed to go into town and the other half was engaged in holiday relaxation, the watchmen flew into the school, pale as death, and waving their arms and gasping with excitement shouted at the top of their lungs:

"Gentlemen! The governor general is in the school! He is coming here."

We froze from fear, because the classrooms were in a terrible, disorderly mess, nothing was where it belonged, and we ourselves were not properly dressed. Some had their jackets off, some their boots; one student had piled one stool on top of another and for some reason was climbing up the wall, hanging onto some iron hooks fixed there. At first we thought it was a false alarm, since we hadn't heard the slightest sound of a carriage driving up to the school, but then a deep bass voice resounded on the staircase, along with the jingling of spurs and the clanging of a sword, and we could no longer doubt that the danger was imminent.

We quickly set about putting ourselves and the classrooms in order, and in this we were quite successful, since the supervisor on duty, suspecting that our situation was not quite what it should be, purposely detained the august visitor on the staircase with various explanations and excuses, thus gaining us some time.

The doors of all the classrooms were flung wide open by the guards, and on the threshold of the first one there appeared the solid and imposing figure of General B., a source of fear for the whole population of the district. Besides the supervisor on duty, the general was accompanied by a short, bent old man with a large bald spot on his head and large gold spectacles on his wrinkled nose, from which protruded long tufts of hair.

Looking more closely, we recognized the old man as the marshal of nobility for the province, Count P.

"Hello, lads!" the general greeted us as if we were soldiers, taking off his large plumed triangular hat.

"We wish you good health, Your High Excellency!" shouted all the students.

We looked at the general. His face was not threatening; he was even smiling. That meant he was in good spirits, and we cheered up a bit, but our hearts continued to pound as they do during moments of danger.

The general, after first explaining something in French in a low voice to the marshal, began to tour the classrooms, going up to each desk and looking at the books lying in front of the students. With some students he entered into conversation, and in doing so his voice sounded unusually soft, kind, and protective. He used the respectful form of address with everyone, a politeness he often dispensed with in his relations with teachers and administrative officers. Coming up to me, he said:

"Your name?"

I told him. He tossed his head upwards and screwed up his eyes, as if trying to remember something.

"Was it you who wrote a play for the theater?"

"Yes, it was me, Your High Excellency," I answered and turned white as a sheet. It flashed through my mind, you see, that he might have come to announce to me the sentence handed down by the military court for the *crime* I had committed. But when he began to tell the marshal in French about the performance we had put on and smiled good-naturedly, stressing our inventiveness and the cleverness we had shown in deceiving the supervisor on duty, I calmed down and cheered up. The marshal, adjusting his glasses and coming up so close to me that I could hear the ticking of the watch in his vest pocket, began to stare straight at me, which made me feel terribly awkward. I lowered my eyes.

"And are you writing something now?" the general continued his questioning.

"I am."

"What?"

"A comedy."

"What's the title?"

"*To Each According to His Deserts.*"

"Who are the characters?"

I listed them.

"No females?"

"No."

"Why?"

"Because I am unfamiliar with the subject."

"Ha, ha, ha!" the general roared with laughter, waving his arms gaily and making a tapping noise with his sword. "Just like you and me, count," he said in French to the marshal, nudging him in the side with his elbow and exchanging with him significant winks. The marshal was known in the town as an indefatigable ladies' man.

"Well, you are a very moral young man," the general said, clapping me on the shoulder and setting off for another classroom, still laughing and repeating my naïve answer. The marshal followed him, but then after a few steps turned around, ran up to me, and, mysteriously, whispered this question into my ear:

"A po polsku umiesz?" [Do you know Polish?]

"Umiem, panie hrabio," [I do, count] I answered, also in a whisper.

"Dobrze, kocham," [Good, I like you] he said, squeezing my elbow and running after the general.[30]

Thus was revealed the secret that I was writing a new play. But I didn't show it to anyone even when it was finished, because when I measured it by the standards of my critic, i.e., the gymnasium student Za***cki, I didn't like it, and without any hesitation consigned it too to the flames. I did the same with all my literary experiments in prose and verse: I would write something, then criticize it severely, and then—burn it to cinders. This way of living the literary life I liked very much.

THE END

Lev Levanda in his youth.
From the New York Public Library Collections.

Translation by Hugh McLean (1995), edited by Conor Daly (2021).

The original Russian-language text of Levanda's novella was first serialized in 1882 over ten editions of the journal *Russkij Evrej*.

Notes *(by Conor Daly, unless otherwise indicated)*

1   *Faust*, by Johann Wolfgang von Goethe (1749-1832), is a tragic drama in two parts, part one of which was published in a number of revisions between 1808 and 1829. The verse cited by Levanda is taken from part one. Gretchen is the short form of the name Margarete, who is Heinrich Faust's love in the work.

2   *Turandot* here refers to the stage play of this name by Friedrich Schiller (1759-1805) written in 1801. Carl Maria von Weber (1786-1826) added an overture and six musical in 1809. Schiller's play was based on the 1762 comedy of the same title written in Italian by Venetian

dramatist Carlo Gozzi 1720-1806). *Kabale und Liebe* [Intrigue and Love], a drama by Schiller, first performed in 1784.

3   Three poems by Mikhail Lermontov (1814-1841), the most prominent figure in Russian Romanticism.

4   *Der Galanthomme Oder Der Gesellschafter, Wie Er Sein Soll* (1842), by Johann Traugott Schuster (1810-73).

5   Special charities existed in many Jewish communities to collect and distribute funds for the dowries of poor girls and orphans. These were called Hakhnasat Kallah societies—from the Hebrew הַכְנָסַת כַּלָּה, "bringing in the bride," that is, bringing her under the wedding canopy.

6   This is a reference to a famous stage direction at the end of the tragedy *Boris Godunov* (1831), by A. S. Pushkin. The boyar Masalsky, one of the murderers of Godunov's widow and her son, addresses the crowd: "People! Maria Godunova and her son Fyodor have poisoned themselves. We have seen their dead bodies. (*The people stay silent in horror.*) Why are you silent? You should shout: long live Tsar Dmitry Ivanovich. (*The people are silent.*)" Marina Mniszech (1588-1614) is the ambitious Polish noblewoman with whom Dmitry, the Pretender, falls in love.

7   Deuteronomy 22:5 "The woman shall not wear that which pertaineth unto a man, neither shall a man put on a woman's garment: for all that do so are an abomination unto the Lord thy God."

8   Sergei Uvarov (1786-1855) was minister of national education under Tsar Nicholas I. The Russian imperial slogan "Orthodoxy, autocracy, and nationality" is attributed to him.

9   During that period the Russian word for "enlightenment" [просвещение] was used in the ministerial title (rather than the currently used term "education" [образование]).

10 Historian Nikolai Ustryalov (1805-70) was close to Minister of Education Sergei Uvarov and was held in high regard by Tsar Nicholas I. Between 1837 and 1841 he wrote *Russian History* (5 vols.), which was used as Russia's sole official college history text book until the 1860s.

11 A celebrated ode by Vladimir Zhukovsky (1783-1852), written in 1812.

12 Abraham Dov Ber Lebensohn (c. 1789-1878), Lithuanian Jewish Hebraist, poet, and educator. He was one of the principal teachers in the rabbinical school of Vilnius for nearly twenty years from 1848.

13 Ilya Gavrilovich Bibikov (1794–1867) had a distinguished military career and was administrative head of the Lithuanian gubernia from 1850 to 1855. This role included management of educational institutions within the Vilnius Educational District. His brother Dmitry served as minister of internal affairs under Tsar Nicholas I.

14 Nikolai Gogol died in Moscow on February 21, 1852, aged forty-two.

15 The reference here is presumably not to either of the famous writers named Tolstoy, Lev Nikolaevich or Aleksei Konstantinovich, but to Count Aleksandr Petrovich Tolstoy (1801-73), a close friend of Gogol's in his later years, who lived in Moscow. Later (1856-62) he served as ober-procurator of the Holy Synod.

16 A work by Gogol with this title was published posthumously in 1855, but it had circulated widely before that in manuscript copies. It was a reply to the harsh criticisms that had been made of his last book *Selected Passages from My Correspondence with Friends* (1847).

17 Translator's comment: Levanda seems to be hinting that the teacher made up his acquaintance with Gogol, but the details given, Count Tolstoy and the manuscript work *Avtorskaia ispoved'*, are authentic and would seem to confirm the teacher's claims.

18 A character in Gogol's novel *Dead Souls*, published in 1842 under the title *The Adventures of Chichikov.*

19 Nikolai Gerasimovich Ustryalov (1805-70), Russian historian.

20 A state-supported organization established in Saint Petersburg in 1834 that sponsored the publication of historical documents, among them the medieval Russian chronicles.

21 Historian, geographer, and educationalist Semyon Smaragdov (1805-71), author of a number of popular history textbooks.

22 Count Johann Tserclaes von Tilly (1559-1632), principal commander of the Catholic League forces during the first half of the Thirty Years' War (1618-48).

23 The Polish military was reconstituted several times between the partition of Poland and 1918. Congress Poland had a separate army from 1815 to 1830, but this army was disbanded after the November Uprising of 1830.

24 Grand Duke Konstantin Pavlovich of Russia (1779-1831), brother of Alexander I and Nicholas I.

25 Ivan Fedorovich Paskevich, (1782-1856), a Russian general who fought in the Turkish and Napoleonic wars.

26 Count Ivan Ivanovich Dibich-Zabalkanskij (1785-1831) was a Baltic German general in Russian service. His family was of Silesian origin, hence the German-language version of his name: Hans Karl Friedrich Anton Graf von Diebitsch und Narten.

27 Aleksander Fredro (1793–1876) was a Polish Romantic poet, playwright, and author .

28 The reference is probably to Józef Korzeniowski (1797–1863), considered one of the major exponents of Romantic drama in Poland, alongside Słowacki, Mickiewicz, and Krasiński. May also refer to writer and sometime-dramatist Apollo Korzeniowski (1820-1869), the father of Joseph Conrad.

29 Wojciech Bogusławski (1757-1829), actor, opera singer, and dramatist—often referred to as the "father of Polish theater."

30 Translators note: Levanda expects readers to understand that the marshal was Polish, while the governor general was Russian. They may have talked French because the marshal didn't speak Russian very well. The marshal wanted these Polish Jews to be Polish, know Polish, but he had to be careful in front of Governor General Bibikov.

On Hugh and a Berkeley PhD: Recollections of Hugh McLean, Translator and Professor of Slavic Studies

Brian Horowitz

In my files I have nearly one thousand letters from Hugh McLean sent to me from before the dawn of the digital age until his death in 2017. He mailed his encouragement to far-flung places: Moscow, Heidelberg, Paris, and Jerusalem; and, of course, Lincoln, Nebraska and New Orleans, Louisiana. The last two were my permanent addresses after I was hired as an assistant professor in 1993 and associate professor in 2003.

In January 1984, I arrived in Berkeley to study Slavic languages and literature, and received my PhD in 1993. Although it would appear that earning a PhD in nine years is hardly a great feat, one should know that I left Berkeley in 1989 for the first of four years of grant-funding to complete my (550-page) dissertation on Mikhail Gershenzon, the Russian Jewish intellectual, philosopher, and scholar of Alexander Pushkin. My thesis advisers were Hugh McLean, Irina Paperno, and Nicholas Riasinovsky.

At that time the Slavic Department at Berkeley was rated number one in the US and was populated with eminences: the Noble Prize-winner, Czesław Milość; the pioneer of American Slavic studies, Francis Whitfield; the genius, Simon Karlinsky; a Tartu School protégé of Yury Lotman, Boris Gasparov; the dignified Olga Raevsky-Hughes; and, of course, Hugh McLean, an American prince who graduated from Yale and then served as a translator for US Intelligence in Germany after World War II.

Berkeley was famed for a curriculum that matched the depth and rigor found in nineteenth-century Europe's greatest universities. It meant an emphasis on language acquisition and bibliographic knowledge. In 1989, one could not get a CAL PhD without four languages: Russian, a second Slavic language (such as Polish or Serbian), French, and German. Only a few years earlier had the university eliminated the need for ancient Greek and Latin. Additionally, one faced the accursed reading list that served as the frame for MA and PhD examinations. The list contained several hundred titles and was around twenty pages in length. It was probably intended as a guide to a lifetime of reading rather than just the PhD. I didn't mind the list, but it haunted others; if a book was on the list, it might be on the exam.

I got to know Hugh in preparation for my MA exams, which were divided into two parts, each consisting of four hours. He gave me examinations from previous years and generously offered to read my answers. His comments were equivalent to a full course in expository writing. I wrote one or two answers every day and he sent back his remarks. Over a few months, I gradually learned the rules of the profession. I recall thinking that graduate school was a place where scholars were born of ordinary men and women.

Interaction with Hugh inspired me. I continued to stay close to him, taking his Kiev Rus' class and then another on Muscovite literature. I still have my set of Dmitry Likhachev's texts with the Slavic on the left and the modern Russian on the right. Although Hugh was not a specialist in medieval literature, he reached a high level of expertise. I also attended his Anton Chekhov course, one of the best I have ever taken. Hugh asked me to grade the student papers and give comments, which I did, although he also graded them to reassure students that their scores did not depend solely on the reactions of a novice.

When it came time for my dissertation, I had planned to write on the Soviet potboiler novel and deal with high and low culture in the late Soviet period. My supposition was that, in addition to dissident literature, low genres were penetrating the literary sphere. I gave an initial paper At UCLA on the novels of Eduard Limonov and quoted directly, often using expletives, which shocked some in the audience. But all the time I kept thinking about a more philosophical topic because I was riveted by European intellectual history—what in America is known as the history of philosophy. For at least three years straight, I spent whole days on the second floor of Café Mediterranean on Telegraph Avenue, where, having bought a few books at Cody's across the street, I read late into the evening and polished them off. On one of these occasions, I fell upon Gershenzon and Viacheslav Ivanov's *Perepiska iz dvukh uglov* (*Correspondence Across a Room*) written in 1922, when the two intellectuals found themselves sharing a room in a sanatorium in Moscow.

Who was Mikhail Gershenzon? I wondered. That question led me to a five-year quest to learn all I could about him through research in archives in Russia (primarily at the Lenin Library), Israel, France, and New York. From various places, I sent Hugh drafts and he sent back comments. His erudition astounded me. From an initial grant from UC Berkeley to go to Leningrad, I received fellowships from the Lady Davis Foundation, the Deutscher Akademischer Austauschdienst, and the Mellon Foundation. Later I would also win IREX, Fulbright, Yad Hanadiv, and Alexander Von Humboldt fellowships. My dissertation "M. O. Gershenzon and Intellectual Life of Russia's Silver Age" was finished in 1992. In 1991, I published my first article in *The American Scholar* and received an encouraging letter from Caryl Emerson at Princeton. I was offered a one-year job at the University of Nebraska in Slavic and Jewish studies, and I became a permanent faculty member the year after.

My relationship with Hugh and his wife, Catherine (Kitty), grew deeper after graduate school. Hugh and I corresponded daily and he continued to critique my work. In addition to Gershenzon, I was writing about Russian philosophical thought, and then moved into Russian Jewish history. It turned out that Hugh also knew a lot about those topics. He especially liked my articles on Mikhail Morgulis, Simon Dubnov, Genrikh Sliozberg, Lev Levanda, and other Jewish intellectuals in tsarist Russia. These pieces later became the nucleus for my book *Empire Jews*.

At some point in the late 1990s, I asked him if he would translate one of Levanda's stories for an anthology of Russian Jewish fiction that I envisioned publishing. He agreed and I chose the novella that appears here. In fact, this is the first full work of Levanda's fiction that has appeared in English. I have to admit that my request caused him some grief because the project was not easy. Levanda is no great stylist and he used lexical items that one could not find in a dictionary. My plan for the anthology dissipated as, ultimately, no publisher was interest in the project. As a result, Hugh's translation sat in my files for more than a decade.

Hugh congratulated me when my books *Empire Jews* (Slavica) and *Jewish Philanthropy and Enlightenment in Late-Tsarist Russia* (University of Washington Press) appeared in 2009. He sent his good wishes when *Russian Idea—Jewish Presence* was published in 2013. I can only say that much of what I was able to accomplish was due to his efforts.

I saw him not long before he died. He took me and my family out for Thai food, as he always did when I came to Berkeley. He and Kitty were fragile, but Hugh spoke enthusiastically as always about the novel he happened to be reading. It was inspiring to meet. We often say, "May his memory be as a blessing." I feel blessed to have known him.

Index

www.ingramcontent.com/pod-product-compliance
Lightning Source LLC
Chambersburg PA
CBHW050129030726
47505CB00007B/2095